BREAKOUT!

"Let's get this over with, Croft," Kyle Garret said as he cleaned off his plate, and washed down his morning meal with the last of his coffee.

"You heard the boss," Croft growled to one of his subordinates, who immediately got up and headed for Will Carston and Bill Hardy.

It was the last thing he ever did.

He reached down to pull Hardy up by an elbow, but before he could grasp the young gambler, Hardy brought his six-gun up into his stomach and shot him once. The shot rang throughout camp and the outlaw staggered back, clutching his stomach in pain as he fell to his knees. He was reaching for his six-gun when Hardy shot him a second time, this time the bullet going straight through his heart and killing him before he hit the ground.

Will Carston rolled to his side, working himself to his knees as he took aim at the nearest member of the Garret crew and shot him twice, too. By the time the shots were off, lead was flying everywhere in the camp. . . .

Books by Jim Miller

Carston's Law
Shootout in Sendero
Stagecoach to Fort Dodge
The 600 Mile Stretch
Rangers Reunited
Too Many Drifters
Hell with the Hide Off
The Long Rope
Ranger's Revenge

Published by POCKET BOOKS

THE EX-RANGERS

CARSTON'S LAW

JIM MILLER

POCKET BOOKS

New York   London   Toronto   Sydney   Tokyo   Singapore

This book is a work of fiction. Names, characters, places and incidents are either products of the author's imagination or are used fictitiously. Any resemblance to actual events or locales or persons, living or dead, is entirely coincidental.

An *Original* Publication of POCKET BOOKS

POCKET BOOKS, a division of Simon & Schuster Inc. 1230 Avenue of the Americas, New York, NY 10020

ISBN: 978-1-5011-0950-8

First Pocket Books printing February 1993

10 9 8 7 6 5 4 3 2 1

POCKET and colophon are registered trademarks of Simon & Schuster Inc.

Cover art by Garin Baker

Printed in the U.S.A.

For Roger, Linda, Shelley,
David, Carrie and Matthew,
who know the true meaning
of friendship and being a good neighbor.

CHAPTER
★ 1 ★

Beat you again, Pardee." young Bill Hardy smiled as he laid down three aces and raked in the pot from his poker winnings. An affable man of nineteen years, he had drifted into Twin Rifles close to a week ago, spending most of his afternoon and evening hours playing cards at a table in Ernie Johnson's Saloon. For the most part he seemed to come up with a fair amount of winning hands. But then he usually bought the house at least one round of drinks during the evening, so not many complained of his prowess with a deck of cards.

"I don't know, Hardy, you sure do have the luck of the draw," Pardee Taylor said with a frown as he looked at the busted flush in his hand. Maybe Will Carston was right, maybe he couldn't bluff worth a

1

damn. At least not at cards, anyway. Pardee was the reformed town drunk and bully. In fact, ever since he'd cut down on his alcohol consumption, he'd found that the people in Twin Rifles were a whole lot more friendly toward him. Why, he even made enough money at odd jobs around town to eat at Big John Porter's Cafe . . . and play a friendly hand of poker once in a while. The trouble was, he was better at eating than he was at the pasteboards. "Damn," he whispered to himself as he fished his big hands through his pockets and found nothing. "Looks like you flat cleaned me out, kid."

He was pushing his chair away from the table when Bill Hardy tossed a coin across the table to him. "Ain't no man should leave a place like this with empty pockets, Pardee," he said with that same friendly smile. "Believe me, friend, I know how it feels," he added. "Been in a fix like that more times than I care to count."

It wasn't the fact that the young gambler had tossed a coin to him that bothered Pardee Taylor so much as what he knew the coin to be—a five-dollar gold piece.

"You sure you want to do this?" Pardee asked, a curious eye cocked at the younger man.

Hardy took in the small stack of coins and bills before him and replied, "Yeah, I want to do it. It sounded like I'd taken your last two bits, and a man's got to live, right?"

Pardee Taylor swallowed hard as he took in those around him. No man liked to be known as taking money that he hadn't earned. It just wasn't done. "Thanks," he said in a humble manner and pocketed the coin. He started to turn away, then stopped, facing the seated young man. "If you're still here in a week or so, I'll be back to win back the rest of my money."

"Wouldn't deny you the chance, Pardee," Hardy said and stuck his own hand out to Pardee, who took it in the friendly fashion in which it was offered, and left.

"Still taking everyone's money, Billy Boy?" Will Carston asked in a few minutes, setting a beer down at Hardy's table, then taking a seat and tabling his own brew. He'd learned of Pardee's bad luck at the poker table when they'd crossed paths at the saloon door.

"That's a fact, Marshal," Hardy said with a smile. "Reckon I'll stick around your fair town until my luck turns."

"As long as you don't—" Will started to say.

"I know," Bill Hardy interrupted, holding a hand out before him, palm facing forward as though to fend off an attack. "As long as I don't start no trouble. Believe me, Marshal, I ain't forgot what you told me when I come into town."

Will glanced at the stack of money before the young gambler and said, "I didn't figure you for being short on memory."

Will Carston had been stopping at Ernie's saloon for a late afternoon beer ever since young Bill Hardy had hit town. He found that he'd enjoyed the young lad's company for the hour or so they would talk. And the young gambler hadn't been a braggart about himself as he talked, each day doling out a bit more of the life and times of young Bill Hardy. So far Will had been able to find out that the young man had been born somewhere up in that area they were calling Nebraska. He'd had a fairly tough youth, losing his parents at an early age and being raised for the most part by a rather rough-and-ready uncle who had lost his wife some time ago and was anything but motherly. Naturally, he'd become proficient with the pasteboards over the years and was now able to make a small living at the poker tables. What he hadn't mentioned—and what Will was perhaps more interested in—was where he'd come from and where he was going, and how good he was with that Navy Colt's he wore on his hip in a cross-draw fashion.

It was getting to be close to the evening meal, and the two were finishing their hour of tall-tale telling, when Joshua Holly burst into Ernie's saloon, looking about as frazzled as if he'd personally come from fighting a grizzly bear himself.

"Will, that you?" he quickly asked, squinting his eyes at the poker table, still not sure he had the right man as he walked closer. "You'd best come to the jail quick, Will," he added, once he was sure he'd found his boss. "Old Emmett just rid into town hell-for-leather, acting meaner than I could ever look! Why, he's—"

"He's madder than hell, is what he is." The words came from the man himself as Emmett pushed open the batwing doors of the saloon, standing larger than life just inside them. Almost as tall as Will Carston, Emmett was an ex-cavalry sergeant from the recent War Between the States, a position he had always been proud of. Other than a good horse to ride beneath him, the only thing left of those days were the Colt's Army-Model revolver he carried and the cavalryman's hat he wore, the front brim turned up and pinned back by miniature crossed sabers. Everyone knew that when Emmett said he was madder than hell . . . well, he *was* madder than hell. And that was that.

"Look like you could use a drink, Emmett," a suddenly nervous Ernie Johnson said to the big man and immediately drew a beer for him.

"I need more than that, Ernie. I need my goddamn horses back!" The furrow he worked his brow into could have been put there by a Missouri mule. Or it could be a war map, as Will Carston had once described the face he now saw.

Will Carston looked at his deputy and the local rancher and said, "Why don't you boys have a seat and tell me just what in the devil is going on."

"I tell you, Will, it's the brazenest goddamn thing I ever seen in my born days," Emmett said as he and Joshua took the proffered seats at the poker table. No sooner did the big man have the words out of his mouth than Ernie Johnson laid two beers on the table for his two newest visitors.

"Do tell," Will said.

Emmett did, but only after he'd drained half the beer in his mug.

"Rode up to my place not more than an hour ago, they did?"

"Who's *they?* How many?"

"I'm getting to it, Will. I'm getting to it."

"All right." Pushing sixty from the north side, Will Carston had learned long ago that having the patience of Job often times paid off more than being in a hurry.

"I was working in the barn, breaking up some hay for feeding. Hell, I didn't even hear 'em ride up. Oh, they was smart ones, I'll give 'em that. Walked their mounts up to the corral, I'd say. Of course, after I seen what they was riding, I reckon walking was all them nags had left in 'em."

"I see." A frown had formed on Will Carston's forehead now, but for the moment it was filled with confusion, not the anger of the man who was talking to him.

"I reckon Greta was the first to spot 'em, for it was

5

her I heard yelling. Told 'em to get off our horses, then headed for the house." Emmett had been married to Greta for nearly two years now, which was about when he'd settled in the community of Twin Rifles. But how he'd come to meet her and finally marry her, well, that was a whole 'nother canyon. "That was what got me out of the barn."

"You mean they come into your bailiwick and up and stole your horses?" Joshua asked in a surprised tone.

Emmett drained the beer mug and continued. "That's exactly what I mean! Saddled three of my best horses without so much as a howdy do and lit a shuck like they was pony riders."

"So there was three of them?" Will asked, finally drawing some useful information from Emmett.

"You betcha." Emmett nodded in the affirmative. "Think I got one of 'em too."

"Oh?"

"Yeah. By the time they was fixing to ride away, Greta had gone inside and grabbed that old Henry rifle off the wall and brought it out. Had the good sense to toss it to me when she seen me coming out of the barn. Only had distance enough to get one good shot at 'em, but I do believe I seen one of 'em riding awful slumped over in the saddle before the dust took 'em all in."

"Why didn't you go after 'em?" Bill Hardy, who had so far been quiet, asked.

"I'll tell you why, sonny. Because they was three armed men and I was one man with a family. Besides, I think I recognized one of 'em afore they got too far away. Looked over his shoulder at me and I caught a glimpse of his face from the side."

"Think you know who he might be?" Will asked,

suddenly more than just curious about Emmett's story.

"Yeah." Here the ex-cavalryman's face turned to one of worry. "If he's anything like I remember, that wasn't just no horse thief who'd taken my horses."

"Oh?" Will Carston said, raising a curious eyebrow of his own.

"No, sir. Fellas, I'd swear that man looking at me was Kyle Garret."

"The man killer?" Joshua asked, his eyes nearly bulging from his head.

"Yeah, the man killer."

Will Carston had a sudden and abiding interest in Emmett's difficulty. What he didn't notice was that he wasn't the only one.

CHAPTER

 ★ 2 ★

Joshua and Emmett were talking back and forth about different stories they had heard about the outlaw Kyle Garret. Will Carston pulled the watch fob out of his pocket and glanced at the time piece, noting that it was nearing the evening meal hour. He also knew that the subject of Emmett's stolen horses needed more than the brief discussion he had heard so far.

"Gentlemen," he said, interrupting the rancher and his deputy after gently placing his watch back in his vest pocket, "I don't know about you, but I'm gonna be down at the community table at the Ferris House if you want to carry on this discussion any more."

"Sounds good to me," Emmett said and finished off

his beer, draining the already empty glass of what few drops that might remain. "Mind if I join you, Will?"

"I'd prefer it," the lawman said, pushing himself away from the poker table as he rose to leave.

Joshua sloshed his hat on and headed for the batwing doors, knowing full well that someone would be needed on duty at the jail. "You just make sure you scamps don't eat the place out afore I git off duty," he said, only half in jest.

"I'll have Margaret bring you a plate of what's on the menu once we're through," Will said with a smile.

"In that case, don't take all night eating," Joshua added. "My stomach's beginning to sound like a he-bear whats come out of hivernation after an awful long winter." Will Carston chuckled as the deputy left the saloon and headed back for the Twin Rifles jail.

"You wouldn't mind if I joined you, would you, Marshal?" Bill Hardy said as he too arose from the now vacant table, scooping up his winnings and stuffing the bills and coins into his pockets.

Will Carston stopped a moment at the request, giving the young gambler a going over, as though he might be under suspicion in some legal matter. Then, with a harmless shrug, he said, "I reckon not." Turning to Emmett, he asked, "Any objections?"

"I reckon not, too," was the ex-cavalryman's reply. "Long as you ain't a part of that bunch that taken my horses."

Bill Hardy's engaging smile suddenly appeared. "I'm afraid I'm not a killer or a horse thief, friend. I've had more luck sticking to the pasteboards than any other trade."

"Then I reckon you're invited," Emmett said. "Come to think of it, with all that money sticking out of your pockets, I may just let you buy the two of us supper."

"It's a deal, gents," Hardy said with a smile, not taken aback at all. But then with what looked like at least a hundred dollars in his pockets, he shouldn't have been.

Margaret Ferris was the owner, proprietor and chief cook and bottle washer of the Ferris House, the one boarding house in Twin Rifles. Along with her daughter, Rachel, she managed to run a fine establishment, serving three tasty meals a day and offering lodging at an accommodating rate. She had survived her late husband, Abel, who had helped found the town of Twin Rifles with Will Carston many years ago and who had died during the War Between the States. And other than his own deceased wife, Will Carston had never seen a more independent woman in his life. Unless, of course, it was Margaret's daughter.

After the death of his wife, Will Carston had taken up residence in the Ferris House, trading off boarding and meals in exchange for a good deal of deadwood he managed to provide on a daily basis for the establishment. Living there over two years, Will had taken a liking to Margaret, now that neither of them was married any more. He just never was much on speaking what he felt, not when it came to women, anyway.

The three men took up seats at the far end of the community table Margaret Ferris served her meals at, the closest customer being Dallas Bodeen, an old-timer close to Will Carston in age. The two men had been friends for over forty years, although neither one had ever kept count. They had shared a youth as mountain men in the Rocky Mountains, then as Texas Rangers once the beaver fur trade had died out in the early 1840s.

"Evening, Will," Dallas said, sopping up the last of the gravy on his plate with a biscuit. Like the true mountain man he had always pictured himself as, Dallas Bodeen would wear nothing but the faded buckskins that seemed to be a part of his body. Oh, he was starting to take on a bit of a pot belly, but for his age, he considered himself to be in right good shape.

Will and Emmett said their hellos, then Will introduced young Bill Hardy to Dallas Bodeen. The old mountain man smiled in as pleasant a manner as he could, although he wasn't sure if he liked this young 'un all that much. He'd heard about him by the third day he'd been in town, Hardy causing more than one man to lose a share of his money to him at the gaming tables of Ernie Johnson's Saloon.

Margaret Ferris waited on the three of them personally, giving Will a more than pleasing smile as she took his order. Will felt the red creep up his neck as he watched the proprietress walk back to the kitchen. The specialty of the day was roast beef, gravy, mashed potatoes and biscuits, and all three men found it a suitable selection. And coffee, lots of coffee.

Once Margaret was gone, Emmett was going over his story about the stolen horses for the benefit of Dallas Bodeen. As it had when he'd mentioned the outlaw's name to Will, Kyle Garret's reputation had preceded him, and Dallas Bodeen's jaw dropped a mite.

"Oh yeah, I've heard of that fella," was his comment when Emmett was through talking. "They say he's stronger than six rows of onions."

"Not if he's carrying one of my slugs around in him, he ain't," Emmett replied with an arrogant frown. After a moment's silence, the cavalry sergeant looked at Will, seated across from him, and asked, "When do you want to saddle and ride, Will?"

From the determination in his voice, Will knew what it was the big man had in mind.

"Why is it, I get the notion you figure that *we* are going out on the hunt for this yahoo?" he asked as Margaret began to set plates of food before them.

"Thank you, Miss Margaret," Emmett said when the plate was placed before him. As he set to cutting his roast beef, he tossed a glare at the lawman to whom he was speaking. "My horses, ain't they, Will?"

"True enough," Will said, cutting into his own roast beef. He stabbed a hunk with his fork and was about to place it in his mouth when he stopped and added, "Of course, it seems to me I heard you tell Joshua and the rest of us that you didn't take after those yahoos because you was a man with a family."

Emmett was not the kind of man who took kindly to being proved wrong. He glared at Will Carston with a good deal of hate. "What of it?"

"Then don't you think you'd better stay with that family just in case this Kyle Garret fella makes his way back here a-seeking you out? You know, doubling back on his trail."

The hate on Emmett's face quickly changed to frustration as he realized the truth in Will Carston's words.

"I know, Will, it's just that—"

"You want to be there when I catch up to this fella and pull in his horns?" Will suggested.

"Actually, I was wanting to be the one who pulled his horns in," Emmett said, a hint of a smile appearing at the corner of his mouth as he chewed a piece of beef. He knew the value and pleasure of eating a hot, home-cooked meal.

"Can't say as I blame you," Dallas said. "I'd not only dehorn the bastard, I'd gore him with his own horns, come to think of it." When the others smiled at his words, Dallas looked at young Hardy and added, "Awful quiet. Ain't you got nothing to say about this?"

Bill Hardy finished chewing his food before saying, "I reckon I could volunteer to go along with you, Marshal, if you're needing a riding pard." The words seemed to stun them all, for neither of them thought the young gambler to be anything close to looking like a fighter. But then most gamblers seldom are.

There was a moment of silence as Margaret refilled their coffee cups and they forked more food into their mouths. It was after Margaret had left that Will said, "Actually, I think I can catch up with this pilgrim by my lonesome, son. Besides, you don't want to break that string of luck you were telling me about, now do you?"

"Why don't you let me tag along with you, Will?" Dallas said in an eager way. "You know good and well I'm a damn good rifle shot, even with these newfangled repeaters. And old Emmett says they was three of 'em, anyway."

"No," was Will's definite answer. "The way I figure it, gents, I'll be riding this outlaw's trail alone. Ary Emmett stays out to his own ranch and keeps an eye on it, that'll leave you and Joshua to watch over the town while I'm gone," he said to Dallas. "Trouble rides in while I'm gone, why, you just grab up one of them extry badges I got in my center drawer and give old Joshua a hand," he added, with a wink and a nod. If there was one thing Will Carston had learned over the years he'd been on the frontier, it was that every man needed to be needed by someone, whether they liked it or not. At the moment, offering Dallas Bodeen the use of a deputy marshal's badge was as close as he could come to making the man feel useful while he was gone from Twin Rifles.

"Sure, Will," Dallas said with a grim smile. "We'll hold her down tight for you, me and Joshua."

"What about your boys, Chance and Wash?" Emmett asked.

"Taken off yesterday to chase up more of them wild mustangs," Will replied. "Oughtta be gone upwards of a week, from what they tell me."

With their plans made, it was an hour later that the four of them split up, leaving Will alone at the community table as Rachel and Margaret Ferris cleaned up after their supper customers.

"Here's a plate for Joshua," Margaret said as she lay a small tray with two plates of food on it before the marshal. "If you're heading toward the jail, you'll save me a trip by taking this with you."

"Sure will, darlin'," Will said with a smile.

Margaret warmed up his coffee and almost turned away to head back to the kitchen when she stopped dead in her tracks and faced Will. Though past the age of forty, she still looked attractive for a woman who had spent most of her life on the frontier.

"Will you tell me something?"

"If I can."

"Why is it you men types all get this damn fool notion that you've got to go out and chase down outlaws and Indians and whatnot and do it all by yourselves? Is it that much a matter of pride?" she asked, her voice getting angry the more she spoke.

"Well, Margaret, I'll admit there's a certain amount of pride a man has to keep up with," Will said, rising to his feet. That one motion stood the lawman a good eight inches taller than Margaret Ferris. And if you asked Will Carston why he'd rather do his talking standing up more than sitting down, he'd tell you he didn't like people looking down on him. "But when you get as many memories as I have . . . well, I reckon it just gets to be a matter of seeing if you can go out there and do it all again by your lonesome, the way you did when you was a youngster. And pride ain't got nothing to do with that. That's pure survival you're talking about when you walk down that canyon."

It wasn't the answer Margaret wanted to hear and the big man's words aggravated her just as they had Emmett. "Men!" she muttered. She was about to stomp off in a huff when, once again, she stopped. This time she set the coffee pot down, grabbed hold of Will Carston's face and brought it down to her and kissed it. She didn't even look about to see if anyone was watching, likely because she didn't really care at that point. "There, what do you think of that?" she asked Will Carston in a manner meant to put him in his place.

You could have knocked the lawman over with a feather, he was that stunned. "Well, ma'am, it says a whole lot," he was finally able to say once he got his voice back. "Right to the point, it was."

Margaret picked up the coffee pot, looked at Will as though she owned him, and said, "And if I don't get a kiss like that in return before you leave tomorrow morning, you'll really be in trouble, mister!"

Will made a mental note that night to stay out of trouble with the chief cook and bottle washer of the Ferris House. After all, the sign above the kitchen said: ANNOYING THE COOK WILL RESULT IN SMALLER POR-

TIONS BEING SERVED. Besides, Margaret Ferris was too good a cook to risk being served smaller portions.

And Margaret Ferris got the kiss she demanded the next morning before Will Carston left to track down Kyle Garret and the three horses of Emmett's that he'd stolen.

CHAPTER
★ 3 ★

There isn't much a town marshal can do once he gets to the outskirts of his town, for that is the limit of his authority. That was why Will Carston thought it came in handy to also be appointed a United States Deputy Marshal along with his position as the City Marshal of Twin Rifles. He could go just about anywhere in the state of Texas and his authority was good. What's more, it was backed up by the Governor of Texas, for it was he who had appointed Will to that duty. In an offhand sort of way, Will Carston enjoyed that flexibility, for it gave him a chance to be able to go further and do more when it came to tracking down outlaws and horse thieves.

He still remembered the words he'd spoken to Margaret Ferris last night about going after men such

17

as Kyle Garret being more a matter of survival than the pride she seemed to think involved in such matters. Oh, there was a certain amount of pride all right, for a man always had his pride to consider in these things. After all, he wouldn't be considered a man if he didn't show the gumption to go after the Kyle Garrets in life. Hell, that was his job, wasn't it? But when you got to be Will Carston's age, there was also the challenge of being able to answer the same derring-do required of him when he was a youngster in such a situation.

Before he left Twin Rifles the next morning, Will Carston had made sure to take Margaret Ferris aside and give her a long kiss that was as good as the one he'd received the night before. He knew she was serious about that kiss too, for it wasn't until he'd given her the kiss that she'd filled one side of his saddlebags with homemade biscuits—still warm, by God!—and about three days worth of food she and Rachel had been up a good share of the night before preparing.

"I reckon there is something to that old saw about food being the way to a man's heart," he said with a smile as Margaret stood outside the Ferris House watching him tighten the cinch on his saddle. But it wasn't just conversing with this woman that had put a smile on his face. Seeing her standing there in a shawl wrapped around her shoulders—for it was indeed early in the morning and still a mite cool—he had to admit to himself that Margaret Ferris was still a good-looking woman. Will had joshed her about her beauty over the years, but only as a man would to the wife of his best friend. Now that Abel Ferris was gone, not to mention Will's own wife, Cora, he had come to admire this woman and the way she had taken care of herself and her daughter since becoming a widow. So when he said, "You look right pretty in that light, Margaret, right pretty," both of them knew there was no joshing about it.

"Why, thank you, Will," she said with genuine surprise as a flush of red came to her face. It wasn't as red as her hair, but it still showed on her. "I didn't think I'd ever hear you say such a thing."

"Look even prettier when you blush like that," Will said with a half-smile and finished tightening up the cinch on his mount. He hated being put in awkward positions where the use of words was concerned, and he said the first thing that had come to his mind, hoping he wasn't making himself look anymore foolish than he already felt.

"Your compliment is accepted and appreciated," Margaret said with a shrewd smile. What she had in mind next, she gave only a moment's thought. One quick glance to see that the streets were still relatively empty in the dawn light, and she made her way down the steps of the boardinghouse and stood in front of Will Carston. Neither spoke for a brief few moments. Neither had to. Their kiss was soft and lingering and when they parted they both seemed slightly embarrassed. After all, this was not an activity one did in public. Even married couples were never seen to display such affection in other than the confines of their own bedroom.

"Well, ma'am," Will stammered, the red now creeping up his own neck and filling his cheeks. "I reckon I'd better be going. Burning daylight, you know."

"Just a minute ago you were kissing me," Margaret said. She was looking into his eyes with the kind of look Will Carston had never seen before, not unless it

19

was years ago when Abel was still alive. "Don't you remember that?"

Will coughed nervously. "Oh, yes, ma'am. I remember it. Fact is, I doubt I'll ever forget it. But there's Abel and Cora to think about too, you know."

"Yes," she nodded, knowing full well what he meant. "I know. But—"

"We'll talk about it when I get back, Margaret," Will said as he climbed into his saddle. No sooner was he seated than Margaret reached up and took hold of his hand in her own.

"Come back to me safe, Will Carston."

"Margaret, I've been coming back to people and places a good fifty some years now," he replied matter-of-factly. "Believe me, this time ain't gonna be no different."

Will Carston turned to leave without another word. At the edge of town, he reined in his mount and looked over his shoulder at Margaret Ferris, who was still standing there and now gave a gentle wave to him. He returned the wave and faced the trail he was about to follow.

"Forgive me, Cora," he whispered to himself as he set out to track down Kyle Garret, horse thief and man killer.

Margaret watched him go, didn't move until Will Carston was plum out of sight.

"Will got hisself a-going, huh?"

She jumped at hearing the words of Dallas Bodeen in the middle of the street.

"Oh, you startled me," she said, bringing a hand up to her throat, as though it would help her catch her breath. "Yes, he's gone."

Dallas followed her into the Ferris House, her first

lone customer of the day. When the panic hit her, she stopped and whirled to face the old-timer.

"Say, just how much did you—"

"Oh, I seen everything, Miss Margaret," Dallas said with a sly grin. "Learned long ago to fit into the shadows right well. Yes, ma'am."

"Then you—" The panic continued to grow as her worst fears were realized.

"Seen it all, yes, ma'am. You and Will exchanging words and . . . and all." He was still grinning mischievously. When he saw the worry in her face, he added, "Oh, but I ain't gonna tell no one, Miss Margaret. No ma'am." The words were meant to assure her but they only seemed to make her mad.

"Listen to me, you old buzzard," Margaret said in a furious manner. "You breathe so much as a word of this to anyone, and I'll fix you good!" It was fire Dallas Bodeen was seeing in Margaret Ferris's eyes and the old mountain man knew it well.

"Yes, ma'am," he exclaimed. "I mean, no ma'am. You won't get no trouble out of me. Swear to God, you won't."

"Then sit down and shut up," she said angrily and walked off in a huff toward the kitchen. At the entrance to the kitchen she stopped and turned once again to face the old-timer. Shaking a vengeful finger at him, she spit out, "Poison you, I will! That's what I'll do!"

Watching her enter the kitchen, Dallas, a sorrowful look about him, muttered, "I surely hope not, Miss Margaret."

CHAPTER

★ 4 ★

Picking up the trail of Kyle Garret didn't prove as hard as Will Carston first thought it would be. After leaving Twin Rifles and Margaret Ferris, he rode out to Emmett's ranch where he was greeted by the big rancher. The two shared a cup of coffee and began to track down the horse thieves. What they did was ride about a quarter of a mile away from the ranch, at which point each man rode in the opposite direction until they had completed a circle of the outlying area of the Emmett Ranch. As long as no torrential rain or big wind had come up over night, this was likely the easiest way to find the trail—or at least the beginning of a trail—the horse thieves might have taken from Emmett's ranch. Will was halfway through making his portion of the circle around the ranch when he heard Emmett fire his six-gun in the air.

"Here they are," the ex-cavalryman said when Will rode up by his side. "By God, they ain't gonna get away from me, the bastards!"

"How do you know for sure?"

"Well, hoss, if that ain't blood, I'll be a monkey's uncle," Emmett said, pointing to a dark red spot on the ground surrounding the tracks. "Told you I winged one of 'em."

Will nodded understanding.

"And them's my horses, bigger than God made green apples," he added with a confident wink. Dismounting, he squatted down next to one of the tracks. "See this shoe? I filed a groove on each side of it when I was fixing to shoe the mustangs. Just in case something like this happened. Yup, that's my horseshoes and them's my horses, Will. Can't ask for better proof by me."

"Well, they're fresh enough, I'll give you that. And if that's how you identify your horses' iron—"

"It is."

Will climbed up in the saddle, adjusting his hat to his head. Looking straight at Emmett, he said, "Then I reckon I got some horse thieves to track down."

"Thanks, Will. Greta will likely have you out for supper some night when you get back."

"I'll plan on looking forward to it," the lawman said and rode off, following the none too hidden trail left by Kyle Garret and his henchmen.

The outlaws made no effort to cover their trail, making obvious stops at whatever watering holes they managed to come upon on their escape route. And at each watering hole Will Carston found a drop or two of blood from the man Emmett had hit. At the end of the first day's tracking, he noticed that the tracks and the horse apples were getting fresher and fresher. It could only mean one thing. The wounded man was becoming a burden to the other horse thieves. At least once the wounded man had fallen off his horse, from what Will was able to tell, so he wasn't getting any better as the day went on.

"Catching up with you, boys," he said to himself when he made camp at day's end, although he could have been talking to the horse thieves themselves from the way he said it.

As much as he wanted to catch up with Kyle Garret and his men, Will's thoughts that night were filled with Margaret Ferris and his feelings for her. He had truly gone into a period of grieving when Cora had died, murdered by the Comancheros in the spring of 1865. Will had been married to her for over thirty years and could remember nothing but good times he'd had with her during those years. Oh, they had gone through some hard times all right, but the good had always outweighed the bad with Cora. He couldn't ever remember her ever really complaining about anything, even when there was a lot she could have complained about. Sweet Cora had dark brown hair and soft brown eyes and a smile like he had never seen before.

Until Cora had died and Margaret Ferris had come into his life.

Actually, he had known Margaret for as long as Twin Rifles had been around, for it was Will and her husband Abel who had founded the little town way back when. He and Margaret had always been good friends just like Abel and Cora had always been good friends. But that was when they were both married. Now each had lost a spouse and gone through a year or two of grieving, as was expected of a widow or widower. The thing was it had been at least five years now since Abel had died and three years since Cora had died. Will found himself wondering if that wasn't enough grieving time for anyone who had lost a husband or wife.

On the other hand, he wasn't all that sure he should be feeling the way he did about Margaret either. Was it possible for friends to become lovers? If so, he had certainly never heard of it. His daddy had gotten married to his mother when both were quite young and that was that. There had been no dalliances for either of them in their marriage. Life was too hard and finding someone to live it with was even harder, if you thought about it. Keeping that person, well, that took some doing when you considered what life on the frontier was like.

Then there was the fact that his mother and father had been a couple for many a year. His mother had never even mentioned remarrying once her husband had died. But then maybe that was the way of women. Will had never in his youth discussed whether or not his father would remarry should his mother die first. And now here he was facing a situation where his own wife had died and the woman he had been a good friend to over the years, who had also lost her spouse, was suddenly making advances toward him in a way he had no idea how to handle. It almost made him chuckle to himself as he thought of his oldest boy, Chance, who claimed he would rather fight the entire Comanche Nation than go courting a woman. By the time he rolled out his blankets that night, Will

Carston realized that he was feeling much the same way himself.

A man with a bullet in him needed medical attention sooner or later. Will had done some doctoring in his time and been worked on by men who had less than a degree in medicine, but when the bullet—or arrow, as the case may be—was taken out and he was bandaged up, he had always made certain to consult a bona fide doctor to make sure he would heal properly. He had learned early on in his career as a mountain man back in the 1820s and 1830s that knowing at least something about medicine couldn't hurt a body.

Take Three-Fingered Johnny, for instance. A tall, lanky sort who had a good sense of humor, he had gone out to check the traps one morning and lost three fingers to a faulty trap. He had bled like hell that day, even after his friends in camp had done what they could to bandage him up. Unfortunately, no one in camp was really qualified as a doctor, and gangrene had set in within the week. They had tried saving him by cutting his hand off at the wrist, but Three-Fingered Johnny had died before the sun set that day. Loss of blood. The nickname had lasted only one week, for obvious reasons. For reasons just as obvious, Will Carston had spent some time with a qualified doctor back in St. Louis when rendezvous was over that following summer.

Whoever it was Emmett had shot was hurting bad by now. With that in mind, it didn't surprise Will at all when, the next day, the trail he was following led to a little town not far away.

The sign on the outskirts was nothing more than an oversized piece of board, with the single word CURIOUS scrawled across it. Except for the two bullet holes someone had shot through the sign, it was no different than any other welcoming sign one might find on the frontier.

Will rode down the main street nice and slow, taking in those who had the gall to stare at him as he did so. Unless he missed his guess, Curious was a town with little or no law and likely a clientele that only the devil himself would find pleasant. Asking questions of an outlaw in a town like this might well get a man killed, so there had to be another way to find out the information he was seeking. And as high and mighty as they sometimes seemed, Will had learned that most doctors had an air of honesty about them. He reined in his horse in front of a general store. A sign painted on the side of the alley way had indicated a doctor could be found at the top of the stairs leading to a small office above the general store. The sign read: J. MILES, M.D.

J. Miles was a smallish man, with slim, bony, wrinkled hands. Will figured him for being somewhere around his age, although the man had a few more gray hairs than Will. The office he worked out of seemed to fit his own size.

"And what can I do for you, stranger?" the doctor asked when Will entered his office.

"Nothing but answer a few questions at the moment," Will said as he pulled back his jacket and revealed the federal lawman's badge pinned to his chest.

"I see."

"I've been trailing some yahoos who did a mite of horse stealing down my way. Fella they stole the horses from claims he hit one of 'em and I've been tracking 'em, finding blood wherever they stop. I was bleeding that much, I'd want to find me a real doctor and get me fixed up."

Dr. Miles took in Will's physique and nodded. "Big as you are, I imagine you would."

Will smiled, taking the comment as a compliment.

"And you're wanting to know if I've perchance treated anyone with a gunshot wound of late," the doctor said.

"That's right."

"If your friend was using a Henry rifle, then yes, I've probably treated him recently." Dr. Miles walked over to a small table covered with a white linen cloth and picked up a bullet Will took to be a .44 caliber conical type used in the Henry. Will examined it and handed it back to the doctor.

"Looks like you've worked on the man I'm looking for," he said. "Or at least one of them."

"He was close to dying when I got my hands on him. Did the best I could, but he's a mite tore up inside. Bullet hit him from the back, you understand."

"I'm surprised you didn't keep him for further observation," Will said without trying to sound demanding.

"Oh, I wanted to, believe me," Miles said with a shake of his head. "But his friends had other plans. Said they had places to go and things to do. But if you ask me, they were afraid their amigo was going to spill the beans to the next lawman who got near him."

"Took him with 'em, did they?"

"That's a fact, Mr. Lawman."

Will smiled weakly. He'd been in such a hurry that he'd forgotten to introduce himself. "Carston. Will Carston." He smiled and offered the man his hand. "Sorry to rush you."

"Don't mention it. Most people I meet in this business are usually sorry and rushed to begin with."

"You didn't see 'em ride on, did you?" Will asked.

"No, as a matter of fact, I heard they'd taken a room over at the boardinghouse. If they're giving their friend a rest, it's a wise thing they're doing."

"And where would this boardinghouse be?"

Will followed Dr. Miles to the office entrance and stepped outside with the man. "Over there, about three buildings down from the saloon across the street," the doctor said. "On the right, see?"

Will nodded and once again offered his hand.

"You've been a real help, Doc," he said. "I appreciate it."

"Hope you're in as good a shape the next time I see you," the doctor said by way of comment as Will prepared to leave.

"Oh? And why do you say that?" Will asked in a curious manner.

"That fella I treated. One of his compadres was identified as Kyle. Always thought it an odd name, Kyle. Ask me, it's Kyle Garret you're going up against."

"Doc," Will said over his shoulder as he walked down the stairs to the boardwalk, "I already know."

CHAPTER

★ 5 ★

If nothing else, at least Will Carston knew that the infamous horse thief and man killer Kyle Garret was not the one Emmett had hit when the rancher's horses were stolen. It was a good thing to know, for if Kyle Garret was as bad a man as most people seemed to make him out to be, going up against the outlaw would definitely be a rough proposition. On the other hand, Garret wouldn't be the first man with a reputation that Will Carston had gone up against over the years. And in the past fifty some years, Will had learned that a lot of the legend about some of the men he'd met . . . well, a lot of it was made up by the man himself. Usually, it turned out to be more myth than anything else. Still, it was always good to know as much as possible about men like Kyle Garret, for some of what you'd hear about them just might be true.

With that in mind, Will Carston checked the loads of his Remington .44 before crossing the street to the boardinghouse Dr. Miles had told him Garret and his men—or at least his wounded compadre—were holed up in. But a thought struck him about halfway across the dusty street, or maybe it was the cautious side of his nature that told him to hold on a minute. He gave a quick glance at the other side of the saloon that seemed to be located in the center of Curious, and spotted what he was looking for. Without a second's hesitation, he headed for the medium sized building about three buildings to the left of the saloon as you faced it.

The sign said CITY MARSHAL and Will Carston found himself wondering just how much help he'd get from the local law hereabouts. There had been a few instances before in his career where the local marshal was as crooked as any faro dealer, and likely making more money than one.

"This how you keep busy?" Will said when he entered the marshal's office. Not even the squeaking hinge on the door woke up the man seated behind the big oak desk.

"Oh, pardon me, mister," the sleepy lawman said in a rather confused state. He spoke in a wheezy, high-toned voice that sounded anything but authoritative. "I mean Marshal," he corrected himself when he spotted the badge on Will's shirt. "Yes, Marshal, what can I do for you?"

Will identified himself and explained why he was in Curious and who it was he was after, none of which seemed to impress the town marshal, a Todd Harlon by name. Ten years younger than Will, the man

31

appeared to be going to seed already, a protruding pot belly keeping him from leaning forward.

"And what is it you'd like from me?" the marshal of Curious asked.

"Thought you might know if this Kyle Garret fella has been in town, or where I could find him if he is," Will said. When the marshal looked befuddled, Will said, "You do keep track of the drifters who come and go, don't you?"

"Oh, sure. Yes, sure do." Todd Harlon's enthusiasm was not contagious.

"And?"

Once again the bewildered look. "Well, I ain't seen him. If he's in town, that is."

"Your town doctor says he heard Kyle Garret is holed up at your local boardinghouse." The words perked up the city marshal's interest real quick. Or was it fear that was suddenly so apparent in his face? "I don't suppose you'd care to accompany me down to the boardinghouse and see if that rumor is true?"

"Me? Hell, no!" So far it was the only definite thing the man had said since Will walked in. Harlon pulled out his pocket watch, glanced at it and pocketed the time piece. "It's past noon, Marshal. You'll have to pardon me now," he said, struggling to get out of his chair. "I usually close up shop for about an hour around noon time so I can get me a meal at the cafe." Then, like a mother hen, he began making shooing motions with his hands. "You'll have to leave now. Come back in an hour and see me then."

Once he had Will out the door, he was on his way to the local eatery.

Will was none too happy with the cooperation—or lack of cooperation, in this case—he was getting from the law in Curious. All he knew was that time was wasting. Hell, Kyle Garret and his men could be saddling their horses right now and making a fast escape. Checking his Remington again, he decided that he would have to confront these outlaws by himself. For the most part he was confident he could take care of Garret and his bunch. The only odd thing he felt as he walked away from the marshal's office was the strange sensation that he was being watched. It was a feeling that could be unnerving to a body if you let it.

The sign in front of the boardinghouse read: SLOAN'S BOARDING HOUSE. It looked to be in about the same condition as the one he'd seen with the town's name on it, worn by too much heat and too sharp a wind passing through, not to mention what seemed to be the standard bullet holes in the signs located in the town of Curious. Apparently, someone had hoorahed this town real good once or twice and the wear on it was beginning to show. Or was it simply that no one cared enough to fix up what needed fixing up?

"I was just about to take the vacancy sign out of the window," a thin as a rail looking checkout clerk said from behind his desk as Will entered the boardinghouse. Either Garret and his bunch were the last occupants to check in—if indeed they had checked in to the boardinghouse—or Will Carston's presence in Curious had preceded him. More than likely the last for the clerk didn't look any too pleased to have a federal lawman in his presence. "What can I do for you, Marshal?"

"I understand a fella named Garret and a couple of his friends checked in here a short time ago," Will said in a stern way.

"Well, I don't know, Marshal." The clerk seemed to like acting sheepish or to know nothing.

"Friend of this Garret's was pretty bad shot up. Come straight from the doctor's office. Doubt you could miss him."

"Well . . ."

Will's frown turned into a glare as he leaned across the desk and said in harsh way, "What room's he in?" His look got the meaning he intended across to the smaller man.

"Two-oh-five. Yes, sir. Two-oh-five," the clerk said, reaching for the key as he spoke. "Upstairs and to your right. Third door on your right."

Will turned toward the stairs.

"Mister." The clerk was pleading now. "Please don't tear the place up."

Over his shoulder Will said, "I won't if they don't."

Will had his six-gun out before he even reached the third door on the right. He flattened himself against the wall next to the door and rapped hard twice.

"Open up in there. It's the law!" he yelled and waited impatiently for a reply. When none was forthcoming, he repeated himself. This time he listened for a possible window being opened. The man might be trying to make good his escape that way.

But he heard nothing.

After one minute of silence, he carefully turned the handle on the door to Room 205. It wasn't locked, which didn't surprise him. He slowly pushed the door open and stuck his head inside, his six-gun at the ready. But there was nothing. Absolutely nothing. The room had an air of silence about it, and with good reason.

The only one in the room was a man laying on the bed, who at first seemed to be sleeping. When Will opened the shade to let some light into the room, he gave the man a closer look. He was indeed the man

Dr. Miles had said he'd bandaged up, that much was obvious. But when Will gave a closer look, he simply shook his head and holstered his Remington.

Downstairs the clerk had a radiant beam to his face as he saw Will approach his desk. "Thank God there wasn't any trouble up there."

"Friend, that would have been awful hard."

"Oh?" Suddenly worry appeared in the form of a frown on the clerk's face. "Just what did go on up there?"

"Just like you wanted. He didn't make no trouble, so I didn't make no trouble."

"Good." Part of the smile was back.

"But then it would have been hard for him to do otherwise."

"Why do you say that?"

"Because," Will said, "the only fella I seen up there was dead."

CHAPTER
★ 6 ★

Will Carston wasn't sure what to do next as he stood outside the boardinghouse. Unless the two friends of the dead man upstairs had lit a shuck, it was still a possibility that they were in the town of Curious. But where? Even for a small town, there were a fair amount of buildings to be covered if Will was to try to find them. And if they kept moving from one building to another at the same time Will was trying to do the same thing, well, it was the equivalent of a chicken running around with its head cut off. It didn't make an awful lot of sense. Yet, he'd come to track down these horse thieves and it wasn't in him to quit. Maybe asking around at the local saloon would turn up a clue as to where to find Kyle Garret and what was left of his crew.

Will was about to enter the saloon when he bumped into Dr. Miles coming out.

"Say, I'm glad I run into you, Doc," he said as the man was about to return to his office. Apparently, he had stopped in at the saloon after talking to Will earlier and was just now going back to work at his tiny office.

"Oh? How's that?" the physician said, raising a curious eyebrow to the lawman.

"You do the autopsying in this town?"

"That I do," the man freely admitted. "What did you have in mind?"

Will explained how he'd taken the good doctor's advice and checked Sloan's Boarding House for Kyle Garret and his bunch and how he'd found the wounded man the doctor had worked on lying on the room's lone bed. "Dead as could be, he was."

"Hmm. He must have been worse off than I figured," the doctor said, his facial expression changing from that of curiosity to a frown.

"No. You likely did a good job patching him up, Doc," Will replied. "It just didn't look to me like this fella died of natural causes or that gunshot wound of his."

"Oh?" Once again the doctor's interest was stimulated. "And what would your amateur prognosis of his death be?"

"Well, a broke neck has always looked like a broke neck to me, Doc," Will said. "I was wondering if you had a few minutes to take a look at that fella and give me a professional opinion of his death."

Without hesitation, the doctor nodded and said, "All right, Marshal, I'll do that for you." Looking askance at the establishment he'd just come from, he added, "I suppose I'll be able to find you here whetting your whistle?"

"I won't be hard to find."

"No," the doctor chuckled as he began walking toward the boardinghouse, "I doubt that you're ever very hard to find, Marshal."

Will smiled to himself and entered the saloon, taking up a vacant spot about halfway down the bar. He ordered a beer and fished in his pocket for a nickel. It wasn't until he came up with the coin to pay for it that the bartender set a glass of beer down before him.

"Trusting fellow, ain't he?" he mumbled to no one in particular.

"Trustworthiness is not one of Jacob's beliefs," a grizzled looking old-timer not far from him commented. He too had been drinking a beer, but at the moment he only seemed to be toying with the contents as he swirled them around in his near empty glass.

"I believe you, friend." Will noticed that the man was dressed much like his friend, Dallas Bodeen. He apparently held the firm notion that he too was a bona fide mountain man, as long gone as that era now was. From top to bottom he was clad in a wardrobe that was compiled of buckskin and beaver pelt. His shirt and pants were well worn, greasy buckskins that one day soon would be on the verge of falling apart. The flat hat he had perched on the back of his head was sure enough beaver pelt. It too had seen many a day of sun, rain and wind—and looked it.

Apparently, the old-timer wasn't the talkative type, for he said nothing to Will's comment.

"Buy you a beer?" Will asked in a friendly way.

"Thought you'd never ask," the beaver man said, a

hint of a smile finally showing at the corners of his mouth.

When the beer was bought and paid for, the old man drank half of it in one draw, set it down and wiped a sleeve across his mouth. "You can call me Buckskin," he said in a more congenial way. "Most folks do." He held out a paw for Will to take.

"And with good reason, I'll bet," was Will's reply, once again taking in the man next to him and his dress. "Carston's the name. You can call me Will," he said, taking the man's offered hand.

The man called Buckskin chuckled at Will's comment. "Ain't that the truth."

"Spend much time here, do you, Buckskin?"

"He spends nearly all day in this place," the bartender volunteered none too pleasantly. Will had the definite feeling this old-timer wasn't all that welcome here.

"Man's right," Buckskin shrugged, a sad expression coming to his face. "Beaver's all gone. Ain't much use for an Indian fighter or trail scout anymore. What else can a man do?"

"True," Will said in agreement, knowing how the man felt, for in a way he held some of those very feelings himself, especially about the old days when the Shinin' Mountains were the place to be and a man could call an Indian his friend instead of having to worry about being scalped any time of the day or night. "Used to work that trade, I did."

"Do tell!" the old man said in surprise. It was always good to find someone who'd had the same experiences you had; better yet to be able to compare stories about where you'd been and who you'd been there with. Will and Buckskin spent a few minutes reminiscing about the good old days before Will was reminded of his real reason for being in Curious.

"Say, tell me, Buckskin," Will said in as casual a manner as he could muster. "You haven't seen any strangers riding through town lately, have you? They'd be on a long ride and likely would have stopped in here to wash away the trail dust."

All of a sudden, Buckskin had a sly way about him. He hesitated, looked down at his beer, then up at Will. "Could very well be, Will."

"You feel like talking about it?"

"Well now, friend, that'd likely depend on what you think it's worth." In a matter of seconds, the man had gone from being on a first name basis to only being a "friend." Will found himself extremely suspicious about the old mountain man standing beside him.

"I don't get paid much, *friend,*" he replied, again fishing around in his pocket. This time he produced a silver dollar, laying it flat on the counter before him. "I reckon I could pay your bar tab for a day or so if you've got some information worth looking into."

Will gauged this man to be about ten years older than him, so when the old mountain man made a swipe at the dollar piece, it was no wonder he found Will's big hand holding his own down to the bar top once he'd gotten hold of the silver. Will hoped he wasn't that slow when he got to be Buckskin's age.

"What is it you're looking for, Marshal?" Buckskin asked, his hand still covering the silver piece, Will's hand still covering Buckskin's.

"A couple of horse thieves I've been tracking, one of 'em going by the name of Kyle Garret." Friendship could wait. Will was all business now.

"Might be able to help you then."

"Is that a fact?"

"Come to think of it, I could point you in the direction of this Garret fella with no trouble at all," Buckskin said.

Will released his grip on Buckskin's hand and said, "Then point, mister."

But before he would say anything, the old mountain man ordered up another beer. Once it was before him, as well as his change from the dollar piece, which he scooped up and put in his pocket, he tossed a thumb over his shoulder and said, "He's back there. In the gaming room. Billiards, he wanted to play, he said."

Will was checking the loads of his Remington as he gave a quick survey of the barroom. There were three or four other customers leaning against the bar and sipping their beers. He didn't expect to find many men there, for it was the work day and any who could afford to visit the saloon daily usually did so in the evening. In the back of the barroom, way in the corner, was one lone man, drinking a beer and playing solitaire in what had to be the darkest corner of the place. All of the patrons looked friendly enough, so he figured all he had to worry about now was Kyle Garret.

He entered the billiard room with his Remington drawn. It was only a little bit better lit than the barroom itself, but it was enough to see who it was he was going up against.

"Just take it easy, gentlemen," he said, knowing he'd taken them by surprise and not wanting any more gunplay than he could avoid. There were only two men playing billiards that he could see and both froze in their tracks.

Once inside he closed the door behind him, at least part way. He never had liked back-shooters and this wasn't the time or place to see if there was anyone in the saloon brave enough to try using Will Carston for a target.

"Now, which one of you yahoos is Kyle Garret?" he asked.

"I'm afraid you got the wrong man, mister," the big one said, his cue stick still in hand. Although the man was trying to sound sincere, somehow Will knew he was lying, knew he did indeed have Kyle Garret in his presence. Besides, hadn't Buckskin said the two men were back here? Or was he lying too?

"No, I don't think so," Will said with a slight shake of his head.

"And how do you plan on proving it?" the big man said. The pleasant look of a man enjoying a game of billiards had been exchanged for the scowl of a rather dangerous man now, Will noticed.

"I think we'll just take a walk out to your horses and take a looksee at 'em. If they've got Emmett's brand on 'em, you're in a heap of trouble, friend." As much as he'd heard about the infamous Kyle Garret, Will Carston had never seen the man face to face. So proving these two were riding Emmett's horses seemed to be the only practical way to make sure he was taking in the right men. Didn't want to arrest the wrong men now, for it wouldn't look good at all. Not at all.

"Just who the hell's Emmett?" the big one said in a tone that matched the look on his face.

"And what's going on?" the second one said, finally being heard. "What is it you think we did? Or didn't do? Think you can explain that, since you're pointing the gun at us?"

"Horse stealing, gents," Will said. "In case you hadn't heard, it's a hanging offense here in Texas. Of course, I'll make sure you get a proper trial and all, but

I'm pretty sure you'll wind up stretching some hemp before long."

Will was about to tell the two to keep their hands away from their guns and make their way out to their mounts, when all hell broke loose.

"I'm here for you, Marshal!" he heard someone yell as the door behind him busted open and slammed into his back. And when it did, it knocked him forward. A cue stick crashed down on his hand, knocking the six-gun from it, at about the same time someone bolted into the back of him, pushing him to the floor.

A shot went off, fired by whoever had knocked him down, followed by a second shot, one that sounded as if it came from Kyle Garret or his compadre. When he looked up, he had a real surprise. Not from the fact that Kyle Garret and his friend were now long gone, escaping out the back door to God only knew where, but in seeing who it was that now stood over him.

It was young Bill Hardy!

"What in the devil do you think you're doing, you damned cardsharp!" he all but yelled at the young lad. Grabbing up his Remington as he got to his feet, he gave Hardy a look that could kill. "And just what the hell are you doing here? Can you tell me that?"

Outside, he heard the thunder of hooves as Kyle Garret and his henchman made their way out of town. Will quickly ran to the back door and tossed it open, straining an ear to hear the direction in which they had fled. When he was sure what direction that was, he turned back to Bill Hardy, who surprisingly enough was still standing where Will had left him.

"Come on, son, let's take a walk," Will said as he grabbed Hardy's six-gun from his grasp.

"Hey, that's mine!"

"Not for a while, it ain't," Will growled. "You're going to jail, Hardy."

"What! What for?" the young gambler asked as Will marched him through the saloon, out on the boardwalk and down the street to the jail.

"Obstructing an officer who was performing his duty," was Will's reply.

"Is there such a law? I never heard of such a law, Marshal. Honest."

Will stuck his six-gun in Hardy's back, pushing him on toward the jail. "If there ain't, son, there ought to be."

CHAPTER

★ 7 ★

New in town, ain't you?" Ernie Johnson said to the man who had just taken a seat at one of his tables and ordered a whiskey neat. He sure enough looked like a city slicker, dressed in his Sunday-go-to-meeting broadcloth suit and matching pinstriped trousers.

"You've got me dead to rights," the man smiled as he downed his drink and motioned for a refill. Ernie poured the second drink and stood there, waiting to see if the man might want the bottle left on his table. But the man simply toyed with the glass of amber liquid. And Ernie Johnson, he took to giving the stranger a quick study while he bided his time.

Like any man who had spent a good deal of time on the frontier, Ernie Johnson had learned that it was usually quite easy to distinguish the difference between the working man and the fancy dresser. The blue cotton work shirt and denim pants were the trademark of the man who had a farm or ranch out here, and the mode of dress seldom changed whether that man was working his fields or visiting town for a friendly drink while the wife did her shopping at the general store.

The businessmen were the ones who wore the thick broadcloth suits that were so hot during the summer months. Still, broadcloth seemed to be the only available material of choice for that type of man if what Ernie saw on a daily basis was an indication. The gamblers, they had a garb of their own that was often beyond description. The man sitting here now looked more like an out-of-town businessman than anything else, although a drummer was definitely out of the question. Hell, the man would have tried to sell him something by now if he were a drummer.

"Would you like me to leave the bottle, sir?" Ernie said after the stranger had spent a few minutes in thought rather than drinking. "I've got other customers at the bar, you see, and—"

"That'll be fine, bartender," the man said and, digging into his pocket, brought out some coins and plunked them down in Ernie's hand. "This should pay for what I'll be drinking. I shan't be long."

"That'll be fine," Ernie said with an engaging smile of his own as he pocketed the change. He turned to go back to the bar, but the stranger took hold of his arm as he did.

"Pardon me, but would you know if you have an Abel and Margaret Ferris in your fair town?" he asked, baring his brightest smile again.

But this time Ernie Johnson frowned, first glancing at the man, then at his hand on the bartender's sleeve.

"Oh, excuse me," the stranger said and quickly released his hold on the bartender.

"There's a Margaret Ferris in town, yes," Ernie said cautiously. "You have business with her, do you?"

"Oh, no. She and her husband were old friends. I was just passing through and thought I'd stop briefly and say hello. You say Margaret lives here. What about Abel?"

"He died during the war, if it means anything to you," Ernie said. It wasn't the superior attitude the gent had that got Ernie to wonder if he should have said anything about Margaret Ferris as much as the fact that the man suddenly had an overly pleasant smile on his face at hearing of Abel's death. It only took him a minute to mull it over as he went back behind the bar.

In no time, Joshua Holly was pulling up a seat at the stranger's table and setting a beer down as he made himself comfortable. The stranger's first response was one of offense as a frown crossed his face.

"I don't recall inviting you to sit," he said rather gruffly.

"Oh, I just sort of invited myself, mister," Joshua said and thumbed his deputy's badge at the man. "No disrespect or nothing, you understand. We just sort of have a small set to with the people passing through town. Let 'em know we're a peaceable folk and don't cotton to no trouble. You understand, don't you?"

"Oh, sure. I'm afraid your trip has been for naught, deputy, for I've no intention of starting any trouble. In fact, I'm rather harmless. I daresay, you'll probably get to like me too."

"Really? Well, we'll get along like two peas in a pod then, won't we?"

"I'm sure." The stranger took a sip of his whiskey.

"Ernie says you been asking about Miss Margaret," Joshua said. "Maybe I can help you out."

"Well then, where does she live? It's been such a long time since I've seen her that I don't know if I'll recognize her." The man smiled again, took another sip of his whiskey.

"Oh, I'll tell you, mister, from what I've heared, why, she's a flower that blossomed way back when and still got her beauty. Yes, sir."

The man seemed pleased at Joshua's words. "Then I'll be more than pleased to see her again."

"You betcha. Seeing old friends is a real pleasure. Believe me, I know what I'm a-talking about." The deputy paused for a second to catch his breath. "You'll find her at the Ferris House, across the street and down to the end of the block there."

The man finished his drink and stood up. "Thank you for your help, deputy. I assure you, it's been a pleasure."

"By the way, friend," Joshua said, also rising to his feet.

"Yes?"

"What'd you say your name was?"

"Oh, pardon me. How rude. Regret," he said, sticking a hand out to the deputy. "Ransome Regret."

"That feller's gonna be trouble," Joshua said when the man had left and he'd returned to the bar for a refill on his afternoon beer.

"Why's that?" Ernie Johnson asked with a good deal of interest.

"Why, didn't you hear him! That man's got a tongue slicker'n possum grease. And they's the worst kind, you mark my words."

* * *

When Ransome Regret asked for a room at the Ferris House, it was Rachel Ferris who checked him in. At first she thought of him as just another customer, but when she looked up and caught the man staring at her and smiling, a slight chill ran down her spine.

"Is there something wrong?" she asked.

"Nothing. I'm sorry. I don't usually do that," Regret said apologetically. "It's just that you're so beautiful."

Rachel blushed as she handed him the key to his room.

"I know it's a little past the noon hour, ma'am, but would it be possible to get anything from your kitchen? Breakfast seems like such a long time ago, or so my stomach tells me."

He seemed to be a very charming man, Rachel thought, and told him it would be no trouble at all to get him a plate of food.

"Just have a seat at the community table around the corner."

Regret thanked her and took a seat, waiting for his plate of food. He was the only one at the community table, the noon hour customers long since gone. And it was Margaret Ferris who brought out the plate of food to him, along with a cup of coffee. She had served so many customers today that at first she didn't recognize him as she set the food before him. In fact, it was as she turned to walk away that his haunting voice struck her.

"Margaret," Regret said in a soft soothing voice. "I've never seen you look so ravishing. You're still so beautiful."

Margaret Ferris stopped and slowly turned, a fear welling up inside her, the kind that comes about when one believes she has heard the voice of a ghost.

"Oh my God!" she said, as she recognized Ransome Regret, even after all these years. Her hand flew up to her face and she said, "Oh my God, it is you!"

As she ran from the room, tears were streaming down her face.

"Mama, what's wrong?" Rachel asked when her mother all but flew through the kitchen door and collapsed on a wooden chair in the middle of the room. But as much as Rachel would repeat the question, all her mother would do is cry. Finally, she placed a hand under her chin and lifted her face to see if there were any physical injuries. There were none. Still, she couldn't understand why her mother could do nothing but sit there and cry like a baby.

First she got her some water, then tried to get her to drink some coffee. It seemed awkward, for it had always been her mother who was the strong one over the years. It was always Margaret Ferris who did the patching up of wounds and the soothing of hysterical cries. But now, now it was she who couldn't get a hold of herself.

It must have been a good twenty minutes by the time Margaret stopped crying uncontrollably. Rachel thought they had to be the most hysterical minutes of her life, for she could do nothing but stand there and watch the poor woman seated before her.

"Mother, what happened? You're white as a ghost!" she said as she knelt down on one knee at her mother's side.

"I can't believe it," Margaret murmured in a barely audible voice. "I didn't think he was still alive."

"Who?" All Rachel could remember was the man who had just checked in and who her mother had served at the community table. "Mr. Regret?"

With eyes red from crying, Margaret Ferris looked up at her daughter and said, "Yes, Rance Regret."

It was a name, but it still didn't give Rachel a clue as to what had caused her mother to go to pieces like she had. She wanted to help in the most desperate way, but if she didn't know what was going on, or what the problem was . . .

Rachel pulled out her own handkerchief and handed it to her mother. She then pulled up a chair and sat down to face the broken woman before her.

"Mother, I want to help. But you've got to tell me what it is that's got you so upset." When Margaret only looked at her daughter with a blank stare, Rachel grabbed the woman by the shoulders and shook her twice. "I want to help, Mother," she said in a forceful way. "I've got to know. Now, tell me, for God's sake."

It was then that Margaret Ferris told her tale of woe, a story, a memory, she had almost forgotten.

He was known as Rance Regret in those days over twenty years ago, when the Mexican War had just begun and Abel Ferris had met Will Carston in the Texas Rangers. The two had become fast friends and were talking about going off to war with the Rangers.

Will Carston had been married to Cora for a while and Abel Ferris was just courting Margaret O'Rourke, a fiery young redheaded woman he was smitten with. Margaret was truly in love with Abel and desperately wanted to marry him before he and Will Carston went off to war. The only problem was that Abel wanted to wait until he and Will returned from the war. He didn't want to leave her here all alone, only to find out at some later date that she was a widow before she'd even gotten used to being married, was his reasoning.

51

Their romance would have been perfect except for one thing.

Rance Regret.

Rance was just as desperately in love with Margaret as she was with Abel and he did everything in his power to try and persuade Margaret of his love for her. He'd send her flowers, but she ignored them. And when he asked her out, she was always going out with Abel. Finally, he had resorted to drunkenly barging in on the few evenings that Abel and Margaret had, often spoiling any romantic feeling either might have worked up to. Which, of course, was exactly what he'd wanted. Finally, in what Margaret could only recall as an act of desperation, he had cornered her late one morning in her barn as she was hitching up the buggy for her parents.

"Finally got you, you little tease," he'd growled in a mean, drunken voice. Later, she was sure he meant to do nothing more than grope her, but at the time his big hands encircled her and he forced himself on her, she was certain he had been attacking her. When he kissed her, she stomped a foot on one of his own, causing him to give out a loud yell that couldn't have been any better than one of her own. It was then that he'd torn her blouse open and slapped her hard across the face, sending her reeling backward until she fell into the hay.

If it hadn't been for Abel and Will coming by to say good-bye that morning, she might have been raped. They had just ridden up to the O'Rourke farmhouse when Rance Regret let out his blaring yell. He was about to have his way with Margaret when Abel came rushing through the barn door.

Abel was tall, nearly as big as Will Carston, and strong as an ox. With one hand he grabbed Regret about the neck and yanked him to his feet, nearly choking the man as he did. Still holding the man's neck, he hit Regret twice in the face. Either blow would have been enough to knock the man unconscious, but Abel didn't stop there. He had in mind killing the man and doing it with his bare hands, hitting him hard more than once in the ribs, breaking several of Regret's bones she was sure. All Margaret could do was stand there helplessly and watch.

It was Will Carston who had saved Abel's life. In fact, he had saved Rance Regret's life too. He broke up the fight, or beating, call it what you will, and slung the unconscious man over his shoulder and carried him out of the barn.

Out of sight.

Out of her life.

"I never did see him again," Margaret said, dabbing a kerchief at her eyes. "Not until now. I'd always thought that Abel beat him so badly that he had died. For all I knew, Will Carston might have done him in, being the good friend that he was, even back then."

"But what happened—"

Margaret knew what Rachel was about to ask and placed a calming hand on her daughter's arm.

With a hint of a smile and the memory of a fine event, Margaret said, "Your father took me by the hand and dragged me back into my parent's house. Then he told my father—*told him, mind you*—that he and I would be getting married that very afternoon. And that's just what we did.

"Your father and Will went off to the war and, thank God, came back all in one piece. And I lived with Cora for the year they were gone."

"Papa did all that?" Rachel asked, a tear rolling

down the corner of her own eye. But it was from a good deal of pride she had felt for the man she knew as her father, not fear or anything else.

"Yes, my child." Margaret smiled and it made her daughter happy to see that wonderful smile she had. "He was quite a man, and I'll not soon forget him."

"What about Mr. Regret? What are we going to do now?"

"I don't know, Rachel." Margaret shook her head in worry. "I don't care to have the man around, but whether he knows it or not, he's taking his life in his own hands just by being here in Twin Rifles."

Rachel gave her mother a confused look. "Why's that?"

"Will Carston has a very good memory, Rachel. You've heard all those stories he tells about what he calls way back when."

"Yes?"

"Well, I don't have a doubt in my mind that the first time Will sees Mr. Ransome Regret, the past will come flooding back to him in no time . . . and he'll kill Regret where he stands."

CHAPTER

★ 8 ★

I tell you, I was only trying to help, Marshal," Bill Hardy pleaded as he entered the Marshal's office of Curious.

"Shut up," Will Carston grumbled. He looked about and saw that Todd Harlon was nowhere in sight. Somehow, it didn't surprise him. Likely still at the local eatery, taking in a long noon meal.

Although Hardy wanted to, he didn't dare get too forceful, for Will Carston was behind him as he entered the Curious hoosegow, his Remington six-gun prodding him from the rear. And the federal lawman was none too happy about the way young Hardy had interfered with his duty. "You seen that Kyle Garret fella. Why, he's as dangerous as they're saying. Don't

55

you agree?" He took a chance and looked at Carston over his shoulder.

"The man was as gentle as a lamb until you gave him cause to pull that pistol of his and start pot-shotting me," Will said, his tone of voice still harsh.

"You mean pot-shotting us, don't you?"

"Oh, shut up and get on back to a cell, Hardy," Will said with an angry growl.

"Now, just what is it that's going on?" Todd Harlon said in that wheezy voice of his as he made his way through the door to his office.

Will nodded toward a nearby cell that now contained Bill Hardy as its lone occupant. "I got a prisoner I want you to keep an eye on for *at least* twenty-four hours, Marshal."

"And what's the charge?" Todd Harlon suddenly had a very worried look about him as he belched. And it wasn't from the food he had obviously just eaten.

"Obstructing a federal officer in the performance of his duty," Will said, still mad about what had happened to him when Kyle Garret was so close to being caught. When Harlon stuttered with the same confusion Hardy had about the charge being leveled, Will went on to explain what the young gambler had done to cause such wrath to be brought upon him. "This lad's a flat-out nuisance, Marshal," Will added, glaring at Bill Hardy when he was through. "You make sure and keep him here at least that long, you got me?" The glare turned to a disappointed frown as he poked a thick finger in Harlon's direction.

"S-s-sure, Marshal," Todd Harlon stuttered nervously. "That won't be no problem at all. No, sir." He plunked himself down in his chair, likely praying that nothing more strenuous than Will Carston's commands would come his way that afternoon, Will thought.

"Hardy, I don't know what in the hell made you see fit to nose in on my doings, but it was dead wrong," Will said, adjusting his hat. "You take my advice, why, when you get out of this hoosegow, you head for parts unknown and stick with the pasteboards. Believe me, in your case, it's a hell of a lot safer. A hell of a lot safer."

With the determination of a man on a mission, Will Carston left without another word. Had he the time, he likely would have spent a few minutes chewing out Todd Harlon for being such a sad example of a city marshal. But he had other things to do. And it was a good thing he left when he did, for he ran smack into Dr. Miles, who was apparently heading for the jail.

"Oh, there you are," he said when he saw Will Carston on the boardwalk.

"What did you find out?" If Will was less than hospitable in his manner, it was because both he and the doctor knew it was business they'd be speaking of and business that Will was interested in more than passing the time of day. A business called murder.

"You were right about the man's neck being broken, Marshal," Doctor Miles said in a serious way.

Will nodded. "Thought so."

"And by the marks on his neck, it wasn't a fall from a high place that broke his neck. A man with mighty strong hands snapped his neck like a dry twig." The doctor took in Will's hands and added, "Yes, sir, mighty big hands."

"Don't even think about suggesting me, Doc. Breaking a man's neck when he's flat on his back or sleeping, that ain't my style. When it comes to killing, I'd rather do a man in fighting a fair fight."

"Yes, I imagine that is more your style. Now, then, is there anything else you wanted to know, Mr. Lawman?"

Will could see that the man was upset, perhaps about Will's own words to him. "Nothing more than wanting to know if I can buy you a beer."

The physician's disposition mellowed some. "That's a lot friendlier, if you ask me."

The two headed back toward the saloon and bellied up to the bar once inside. Will was silent, but the good doctor had found something else to talk about.

"Say, aren't you wanting to be on your way to finding that Garret outlaw?" he asked as they waited for their drinks. "When I looked for you here earlier, they'd said the man had gotten away from you. And as I recall, you were a mite more than anxious to get him in your sights."

"True enough, Doc, but it's gonna be late afternoon here pretty quick, and truth to tell, I ain't had a home-cooked meal in a few days or a warm bed to sleep on," Will said with a hint of a smile appearing at the corner of his lips. "Besides, my horse is needing some rest too. And these yahoos, why, they got an easy enough trail to follow." Will didn't think he'd mention how it was their trail was easy to follow, lest someone hear him and that someone happen to be a friend of Kyle Garret. In fact, he now found himself feeling less than trustworthy toward some of the people in this town. "Then again, maybe I'm getting old."

Dr. Miles smiled at the lawman's words, running a delicate hand through iron gray hair. "I know what you mean, Marshal."

The two held a friendly conversation for the better part of half an hour before the doctor finished his beer and excused himself. "I'd better be getting back to my office. This is a small town, but it's been my experience that when things happen, things happen."

Dr. Miles wasn't gone but five minutes before Buckskin, the grizzled old mountain man, took his place at the bar. When he silently smiled at Will, the lawman noticed that more than a few of his teeth were either rotten or close to falling out. The old-timer definitely didn't have to worry about being caught by a woman in the marriage trap, not unless she was a truly desperate one.

"Drink up that whole dollar's worth of beer I give you, old-timer?" Will asked, even though he wasn't all that much of a spring chicken himself.

"Oh no. Still got a mite left," Buckskin said, the smile now gone. As though to prove his point, he tossed a nickel on the bar top, hesitated a moment and tossed a second coin on the bar top. "Jacob, let's have a couple of beers for me and my friend here."

Will didn't know if he was showing off or being sincere, although he suspected the former. "Thanks," he said when the beer was set before him.

"Now you can't say I never give you nothing except a hard time," the mountain man said.

"I'll bet."

"Still on the trail of that outlaw?" was the old-timer's next question.

"That's a fact." Will took a long pull on the beer, wiped his sleeve across his mouth, much in the manner of the old mountain man. "What's it to you?"

"Nothing." After a few moments of silence, he added, "Just thought you could use some company."

"Nope."

"Then maybe a mite of help bringing the old galoot in. How 'bout that?"

Will looked Buckskin straight in the eyes and frowned. "Weren't you here when that Hardy boy come busting in on me a while back? Didn't you at least hear what happened in that fracas?" Will said, the anger returning in his voice as he remembered the incident. Hell, he seriously doubted that he would tell it to his sons, much less his grandchildren years from now. "Do you honest to God think I *want* a partner in this trackdown I'm on?"

"Why shoot, Marshal, that boy was a pure Dan'l Boone!" the old-timer proclaimed. "Me, I been tracking Injuns longer'n that lad's been alive, and you know it!"

"No thanks, Buckskin," Will said adamantly. "I've got enough trouble keeping track of what I do alone. Don't need a partner in my law enforcement life. None at all."

Will drained the brew, placed the glass on the bar top, and glanced at Buckskin.

"Thanks for the beer, hoss," was all he said.

Then he walked out of the saloon in total silence.

Will took a room at Sloan's Boarding House and settled for an early supper that afternoon. Afterwards, as evening approached, he asked a few more questions as the sun set, and turned in early.

The next morning he was up early, as he always was, even before the sun began to crack the eastern horizon. He was the first and only customer at the local eatery when it opened and ordered his meal.

"Don't mind if I join you, do you?" Buckskin asked, setting his coffee cup down and taking a seat across from Will, as though the answer would naturally be a yes.

"Looks like you are, whether I want you to or not," Will said, sipping his own coffee. When Buckskin had placed his order with the waitress, a shy young thing a bit on the skinny side, Will said, "This one of your regular haunts, is it?"

Buckskin chuckled, more to himself than anyone else. "Considering it's the only eatery in town, I reckon you could say that. Hell, it's eat here or fix your own possum, and I've had more'n my share of them."

Will knew what the man meant, but he wasn't about to acknowledge the comment with a friendly remark. Hell, he didn't want this man as a friend, a saddle pard or anything else. All he wanted was to get on with tracking Kyle Garret, the horse thief.

He ate his flapjacks, scrambled eggs and fried potatoes in relative silence, the only thing on his mind being the thought of how far he'd be able to get today tracking this outlaw. If he could start early enough, he might be able to catch up with Garret and his friend before sundown and have the two of them in custody. When he finished his coffee and stood up, he was surprised to notice that Buckskin was making the exact same motion, he too being done with his meal.

"Ain't gonna fight me to see who pays for the meal, are you?" Will said as Buckskin stood by and the lawman fished a coin from his pocket.

"You can get reimbursed for your meals, ary I'm not mistaken," the weathered old man said with a sly expression. "Me, all I'm a-gonna get is an empty pocket." He physically patted the pockets of his shirt. "Fact is, they appears to be empty now."

"My Cora would have called you a real scoundrel, hoss."

Buckskin smiled knowingly. "I gauge she'd call me worse than that ary she ever met me."

Somehow, Will knew he'd find what he saw outside of the eatery. He'd tied his horse and all his gear to the hitch rack out front, so far the lone rider on the streets of Curious. But when he left the eatery, sure enough, there was Buckskin's horse and equipment, ready to ride.

"And what in the devil do you think you're doing?" Will immediately demanded. "I told you yesterday, I don't want you with me, Buckskin."

"Oh, it ain't that. Tain't what you think at all." The old mountain man untied his reins and mounted up before speaking again. "Why, I'm just a-leaving Curious. Had my fill of the place, I have. Time to move on, I tells myself last night. Yes, I did."

"And which direction are you headed in?" Will said with a groan as he mounted his own horse.

"Same one you're going in, of course," the man said as though his words made perfect sense.

Will reined his horse to the left and headed out of town, followed at a slow trot by Buckskin. Over his shoulder, he said, "I told you I don't want you with me."

Buckskin pulled up alongside him and, in a desperate tone, said, "But I know where he is. I know where you can find Kyle Garret."

But Will Carston wasn't having any more of this man's tall tales today. Kicking his horse's sides he said, "I don't care if you can find me the Northwest Passage and the Holy Grail and all it's glory. I don't want you!"

"I can find 'em, by God! All three of 'em if I have to!" Buckskin yelled right back and kicked the sides of his own horse.

It was two hours later that Todd Harlon fed Bill Hardy a meal and kicked the door open to his cell.

"That federal man said to keep you in lockup for

twenty-four hours, but I never could keep a body in one of them cells for more than a night, especially the drunks," the marshal wheezed with a bit of difficulty. "Now, I'm gonna let you loose, sonny, but you gotta promise me one thing."

"Anything, Marshal. Anything." After spending a night on the lumpy cot, Bill Hardy couldn't agree with the lawman more about staying in the lockup for more than a night.

"I hand you this here pistol, you gotta promise me you're gonna vamoose. I'm talking about getting outta this town, you understand. But most of all, I'm talking about leaving that federal lawman alone. I don't want to see him around here any more at all."

"Anything you say, Marshal," Hardy said, vigorously pumping the lawman's hand in thanks. He holstered his six-gun, sloshed his hat on his head and was headed for the door.

"And you stick to them pasteboards like the marshal said," were the last words the lawman had for him as he left.

Just to make sure it looked right, Bill Hardy saddled up and rode out of town in the opposite direction the livery man said Will Carston had left town. Then he circled the town of Curious until he was on the far side of town.

Which was where he picked up Will Carston's trail.

CHAPTER

★ 9 ★

Margaret Ferris had an attitude the next morning that was pure business as she went about preparing the breakfast meal for her customers. She and Rachel had sat up the night before and talked about Ransome Regret and how they would handle him. So far they had decided that they would tolerate the man and his behavior and see what happened from there. Margaret set a plate of food before him as though he were some kind of stray dog eating left-over scraps. And if she didn't smile as she did so, it was likely certain that Regret knew why.

After breakfast, Ransome Regret roamed into the room off the dining room that Margaret kept for those who read for relaxation. Here he produced a book and sat down to read it. The fact that he seemed to enjoy it began to bother Margaret and Rachel as the morning wore on.

"Just what is it you want, mister?" Rachel asked him quite bluntly late that morning. Her temper was beginning to boil as she continued to watch Regret sit there and enjoy himself. For the harm he was causing her mother, she wanted to tear the man apart limb from limb.

Ransome Regret closed his book and smiled up at her. "Why, I'm just passing through, my dear girl," he said in an innocent tone. "The same as many a man in this country." Lifting the book in his hand, he added, "I'm also catching up on some of my reading. That isn't a crime, is it?"

"No, but—"

"Then why not simply let me go about my reading and you can get back to your work." The smile that accompanied the words gave off a superior air, one which Rachel did not like.

"How about if I give you back the money you advanced us and you can move on?" Rachel said, sounding close to desperate in the tone of her voice. At the moment she wasn't sure how else she could get rid of this man, this troublemaker.

"Oh, no. Please don't do that, Miss Rachel," he said, once again using the charm of his smile. "I wouldn't want to make a mess of your books. Besides, I'll only be here for another day or two." He was silent for a moment as he went back to his place in the book on his lap. "Honest, Missy, I'm not going to hurt. Honest."

With that comment, Rachel stormed off in huff, not sure what to make of the man or his words. All she knew was that he had upset her mother something fierce yesterday and now he seemed to be doing the same thing to her. She hoped he knew that all the charm in the world wouldn't get her under his spell, whatever that was. Not on your life!

The morning came and went as the Ferris women continued their daily routine of baking and cooking, and Ransome Regret continued to read his book. The only contact he had with them after Rachel's confrontation was a charming smile to either or both of the ladies at midday as they served the noon meal to their customers. But Margaret and Rachel simply ignored the man and any of his gestures.

It was after the noon meal was served and most of the customers were gone that Joshua came in to get his meal. This wasn't unusual at all, for he and Will—or whoever was sitting in as acting marshal of Twin Rifles—would switch off and take their meals whenever it was possible. And Margaret and Rachel Ferris never complained about making up an extra dish after everyone else had eaten and left.

"Looking a mite bothered, you are, Miss Margaret," the deputy commented as he took a seat and she took his order.

"It's nothing, Joshua, I've just got something on my mind," she said, trying her hardest to put up a brave front.

It was after Joshua had finished his meal and Margaret had refilled his cup with coffee one more time that she set her coffee pot down and decided to find out what it was Ransome Regret wanted from her and her daughter here in the community of Twin Rifles. She'd gotten awful sick of Regret's smile, for it now looked more like a leer than anything charming she had ever seen. She walked over to Regret, who was seated across the room and in a corner chair.

"All right, Rance," she said in a whisper she hoped

only he would hear. "Just what the devil is it you want here? What did I do to deserve having you come into my life again?"

In a voice that was just as low, Regret smiled and said, "Why, I thought you'd know by now, Margaret."

"If I knew, I wouldn't be asking you like this, would I," she said, again trying to keep the conversation as private as possible.

"I never did stop loving you, you know," he said. "Even after Abel nearly beat me to death. Even after you got married and he went off to war." The smile widened, taking on what she thought to be a good deal of joy, as he added, "I came to finish what I started with you over twenty years ago, Margaret. That's what I came for."

Once again panic began to fill Margaret at the thought of what he might do, of that horrible memory so long ago. Would he dare try such a thing here in Twin Rifles? Was he insane enough to think she would let him have his way with her now, especially when she declined so long ago? Did he really think she had changed that much? If he did, he was wrong. But that still didn't keep her hand from involuntarily going to her mouth and covering it.

"Is they anything wrong, Miss Margaret?" Joshua said, appearing out of nowhere.

"Believe me, deputy, there's absolutely nothing wrong," Regret said, trying to be engaging.

But Joshua wasn't tactful at all, and it was a mean look he tossed at Regret. "I wasn't asking you, mister, I was asking Miss Margaret."

"No, Joshua, there's nothing wrong. Nothing I can't handle." As much as she tried to maintain control of herself, her hand was shaking ever so slightly. Joshua noticed it.

"Are you sure?" the deputy asked, still pressing the matter. " 'Cause if they is, why, you just a-tell me and I'll take care of it. If this here yahoo's bothering you, just give me the word and I'll have him in a cell across the street quicker'n you can shake a finger at him."

Regret acted taken aback. "Deputy, surely you can't be suggesting that I'm the cause of any trouble. Why, just ask the woman. I've been sitting here all morning, doing nothing but reading. Besides, I thought you and I were getting along famously."

"That right, Miss Margaret?"

"Yes, Joshua. He's been sitting here reading, just like he says." The deputy lawman could tell that, even though she spoke the truth, the words had come out harder than she would have liked.

"There, Joshua, see? Just like I said." The man was acting too innocent, too cocky to suit the deputy. The truth was, he was beginning to dislike this man a great deal.

"Well, that may be, mister, but they's a couple of things we need to get straightened out here."

"Oh?"

"Yeah." Here Joshua's face and tone of voice took on that of a low, angry growl. He leaned down toward the man in his seat, cocking a bulging eye at him as he spoke. "First off, the only one who's gonna be gitting along here is gonna be you ary you ever lay a hand on this woman here. Understand?"

"But—"

"But, my ass!" Joshua glanced briefly at Margaret. "Begging your pardon, ma'am." To Regret he said, "And as for famous, why, I doubt if you got any fame further than being on a wanted poster from back wherever it is you come from." He concluded by jabbing a short, stubby finger at the seated man and saying, "And that, mister, is that!"

Then he was gone, not waiting to hear whatever it was Ransome Regret might have to say. But Margaret felt good about the whole situation. Most likely, she thought, the man is too flustered to think of anything to say. And she too marched off and tended to her business.

"Rachel?" she said as she entered the kitchen.

"Yes, ma'am?" her daughter said, kneading bread.

"Next time Joshua comes in for a meal, give him an extra portion of food."

Rachel looked up, confused. "Why? He isn't that skinny, is he?"

Margaret looked at her daughter in a warm way and said, "Let's just say it's repaying a kindness with another kindness."

CHAPTER

★ 10 ★

Light and sit, ary you've a mind to," Will Carston said when Buckskin came moseying up to the dry camp he'd made the noon of that first day he'd left the town of Curious. He'd followed the trail of Kyle Garret at an easy pace, knowing that as long as the man still had Emmett's horses there would be no problem in keeping track of him. But every once in a while he'd look at his back trail and there was that old reprobate, Buckskin. He was like that all morning, lingering back about a mile or so but just within sight. "Ain't much but that's noon camp for you."

Buckskin dismounted and took in Will, half squatting and half sitting on a rock protruding from the ground, his canteen in one hand, a biscuit in the other. "That the only one of them you got?" he asked, gazing at the biscuit the way a buzzard took in the sight of a dead body before swooping down to feast on it.

Will reached inside the pocket of his buckskin jacket, produced a second biscuit and tossed it to the mountain man, smiling as he did.

"Sweet-talked that young lady at the cafe out of a handful of these before we left," he said and went back to nibbling on his biscuit.

Buckskin got his own canteen and squatted down opposite the lawman. Pushing the beaver hat back on his head, he took a pull on the canteen and broke open the biscuit, eating half of it at a time, as though the process would draw out the meal. The idea was to make it seem like a bigger meal to your stomach. Or maybe it was just the idea of fooling yourself into believing that you were eating a feast rather than experiencing a famine. Whatever the case, it was obvious that both men had been through this type of ordeal before.

"You know, hoss, you could make a man mighty nervous riding back there like you been doing," Will said when he'd finished the last of his biscuit and put the cap back on his canteen.

"Bother you, did I?" The old mountain man said it with a sly smile of his own now. It was as though his intent was to get the better of this lawman and he was succeeding.

Will frowned as he said, "Matter of fact, it does, you old hardhead." The frown deepened and he added, "So if you've got a place to go, I'd appreciate it if you'd git on down the trail and go to it. Me, I got places to go to, and I still don't want no partner when I get there. Understand?"

"Oh, sure," Buckskin said, trying to sound agreeable to Will. "I understand exactly what you're saying.

Don't want this old body around. Well, I ain't gonna be the one to git in your way, Marshal. Not me, not a-tall."

He got up, put his canteen away and mounted his horse. "Thanks for the biscuit," he said, reining his horse to the side. He did something strange next. Tipping his hat, as though he were some grand country squire, he said, "And a good day to you too, sir."

Then he was gone, riding ahead of the trail Will knew he'd be following. And he kept on riding until Will could no longer see him. Then and only then did Will mount his own horse and begin to once again track Kyle Garret and Emmett's horses.

The tracking went easier that afternoon, and a bit faster too, Will thought. For the most part, the land he covered was fairly flat and desolate, although clumps of trees could be seen here and there and the water seemed to be plentiful in the area. The sun shone, giving him a good indicator of the time he had spent and the time he had left to track that day. He thought he made good use of it, even if he didn't catch up with the horse thieves.

But he was in for a surprise when, late in the afternoon, he thought he smelled smoke from a fire. His sense of smell hadn't betrayed him when he soon rode up to a clump of trees near a water hole. And there, with a fair sized rabbit on a spit and coffee on the fire, sat Buckskin. He gave Will the kind of smile that said I-can-do-that-too. It was just that he had more to offer than Will had at noon.

"Light and sit, ary you've a mind to," Buckskin said in a courteous manner.

"Seems to me I've heard those words before," Will said as he dismounted and tended to his horse, loosening the cinch and letting the horse have a good blow.

"Musta been the echo in that canyon nearby," the mountain man said with a wide grin. He was definitely having fun at this game he was playing with the lawman.

Will didn't reply, instead shaking his head silently and leading the horse off to the water hole. As he did, Buckskin made a big production out of slowly turning the spit and basting the game with an imaginary sauce.

"Coffee's biled, help yourself," the old-timer said when Will was through with his horse. A decent man knew enough to take care of his horse before himself, for it was the horse that had been taking care of him all day.

"Thanks." Will took a proffered cup and filled it with the black stuff. It sure tasted good after going since morning without some. He sipped the coffee in silence for a while until Buckskin spoke up.

"Got a knife, you go ahead and cut you some of this meat. Looks done to me," he said.

"Thanks." Will pulled out his knife and did as he was told, cutting a piece of the meat and wolfing it down ravenously.

"Here." Buckskin tossed him a biscuit, much to Will's surprise. When the mountain man saw the look of surprise on Will's face, he said, "You ain't the only one can charm the ladies, friend. Why, I was at the back door of that cafe a half hour afore you even got there. Got me a saddlebag full of these things."

"You pretty much had a set mind about coming along with me, didn't you?" Will said between bites of food.

The old man nodded. "Pretty much. You git to be old as me, why, you git set in your ways real easy."

They finished the meal in silence, neither wanting a cold meal, knowing that hot meals were hard to come by on this frontier. It wasn't until Buckskin poured both of them one last cup of coffee that Will spoke.

"You serious about being able to find Kyle Garret?" he said, "or was that just bluff and bluster?"

"Your horse tracks run out or he takes hisself another horse, I'll find him, you betcha." The old-timer spoke with a wink and a nod, as though to inspire confidence in his words. When Will cocked a curious eye at the man, he continued. "I was following the trail you was following this morning, remember? I can spot a marked shoe as well as anyone, I reckon." So he had found out what Will had meant when he said Garret's trail was easy enough to follow. He'd discovered the marked horse shoe Emmett had put on his mounts. "Hell, it was how I got this far this afternoon and knew you'd be stopping here along the way."

Will didn't say anything, silent in his own thoughts the rest of the evening, until he rolled out his bedroll. It was then he gave Buckskin a hard glance.

"Better get to bed, old-timer," he said in an authoritative voice. "We're riding out at sunrise."

Buckskin smiled that crafty smile of his again. "I thought you'd say that."

They rode together for another day and a half, Buckskin letting Will be the leading force in this expedition, although he secretly knew that he was as much a leader as the lawman he was with. The farther they went, the fresher the tracks and the horse apples got each time they stopped to examine them. Both men knew they were getting close to Kyle Garret and his riding compadre.

It was approaching noon of the third day, by Will's estimate, that they came upon a grassy knoll that overlooked what seemed like a peaceful valley below. In particular, it overlooked a medium sized farm house, with a big red barn and horse corral near it. It couldn't be more than a half a mile away, he thought.

"You stay here with the horses, Buckskin," Will said as he dismounted and pulled his Henry rifle from its saddle scabbard and jacked a round in the chamber, slowly letting the hammer down.

"You sure, hoss?" The old mountain man would have readily volunteered to be a part of any fighting about to take place, Will thought, but he also knew that the old-timer might not know what he was getting into down there, either.

"I'm sure. Catching this yahoo is my job, not yours. You'll be doing me a big favor by just making sure this horse of mine stays put."

Buckskin shrugged. "If you say so."

Cautiously, Will made his way down the knoll and toward the barn, following the tracks of Emmett's horses all the way. The tracks led to the barn, where the horses now stood, riderless. And there were no horses in the corral, so maybe they were in the stalls in the barn for some reason or another. Unless, of course, they were out to pasture. But this looked like a working place, meaning they most likely weren't here at all anyway, this being the middle of the day and all. Still, Emmett's horses were ground tied outside the entrance to the barn, so it was there Will made up his mind he'd go. It was when he noticed that there were no saddles on the horses that he was certain Garret and his friend were in the barn. Most likely, Emmett's horses had played out by now and Garret and his friend were in the process of stealing another pair of mounts. After all, this seemed to be their stock and trade.

He moved up alongside the barn, slowly sliding along the side of the barn door to the entrance, a sudden chill running down his spine, sending a feeling of fear racing to his brain. At first he was unsure what to do in this situation, for he didn't know where the horse thieves were inside. Did they know he was out here? Were they hiding in wait behind a stall or up in the hay loft? And how well were they armed? When he heard a voice inside, he felt a sigh of relief, even if it was only a slight one.

"Where do you think he's at, Kyle?" Garret's companion asked his boss.

"I don't know, all I can see is that old trapper up on the rise. Give me that rifle of yours and I'll see can I knock him out of the saddle," was Garret's reply.

It was then Will went into action. He could tell by hearing the voices that these were the two men he'd encountered in the gaming room back in Curious. With his Remington six-gun in his right hand and his Henry rifle in his left, he decided it was time to do something. Time to keep Buckskin from getting bush-whacked.

Jumping out in plain sight like he did surprised the horse thieves as much as it did Will. It worked to his advantage too for it gave him a split second to glance around inside and see where the voices were coming from. But it was when he heard the lever action of a rifle that he brought his Remington up and pointed it straight at the sound, even though he couldn't quite see who was behind the weapon.

"Don't do it, son!" he all but yelled. "I ain't in the killing mood at the moment, but ary I hear you make another sound, I'm likely to change my mind real quick. Now drop it." At the same time he spit the words out and threw down on the man to his right front, he'd brought the Henry to bear on the stalls on the other side of the barn.

He didn't hear the clatter of a rifle falling to the ground, but he didn't hear any other movement either. For a moment it bothered him and he heard himself yelling, "Damn it, I said drop it!"

The rifle fell to the ground, as did another weapon across the barn floor.

"That's better," he said, his eyes quickly focusing on the inside of the barn and the men he had encountered. "Now you two pilgrims get out here in the open where I can see you. And don't try nothing funny. I ain't developed much of a sense of humor trailing you two."

The two did as they were told, each coming out from behind the stall on his side of the barn. Both also had their hands high in the air.

Suddenly, Will felt something go sour in the pit of his stomach, as though an omen had come to him that things were not all they should be.

Behind him he heard the sound of someone else. He didn't have to wait to find out who it was.

"Say, vot goes on here? By Got, I vant to know." It was an authoritative voice, and with it came a thick German accent. Likely, it was the owner of this farm. But it was who he heard speak next that threw him.

"Finally got 'em, did you, Marshal?" Will gave a quick glance over his shoulder and sure enough, there he was—Bill Hardy! Beside him was the apparent owner of this farm, a dangerous looking pitch fork in his grasp.

It was all the distraction the horse thieves needed, and they took advantage of it. Garret's riding pard took one hasty step toward Will, swinging a long arm out and knocking the barrel of the Henry rifle aside, throwing Will a mite off balance as he did. Then he cut and ran out the back of the barn.

Kyle Garret took that moment to reach down and grab up the rifle he'd been holding before he too broke for the back door of the barn.

But Will had recovered his composure by then and snapped off a quick shot at the man before he got out the door. It sounded like his bullet hit flesh as Kyle Garret disappeared out the door.

"You stay put!" he growled at Hardy before running toward the back door to the barn.

He heard the gallop of horses' hooves before he reached the door, knew the men he was chasing had already saddled and ridden hell-for-leather away from here. His eyes quickly scanned the horizon as he stepped outside the back entrance. He was just raising his rifle to take aim at Garret in the distance when he heard a rifle crack that sounded as though it had come from his rear. By God, it sounded like an old Hawken rifle!

It was when that thought ran through his mind that he knew the rifle had indeed been fired by Buckskin. Seeing Garret's riding pard jerk in the saddle a second or two after he heard the report of the shot made him feel a mite better about those two yahoos again getting away from him.

Will holstered his Remington as he did an about

face and headed back inside the barn. He had the look of a determined man as he focused a mean stare on young Bill Hardy, steadily walking in his direction. He was no more than six feet away from the lad and taking one last stride when he lashed out at the young gambler with a wide swing that caught Hardy right on the jaw and knocked him ass over teakettle. The young man lay there unconscious for a moment as Will found a half-full bucket of water and tossed it in his face.

"Hey! What did you do that for?" the lad immediately demanded in a foul mood.

Will glanced at the empty bucket and said, "I figured you'd need to cool off once you come to."

"Not that! What did you hit me for?" Still unsteady, Hardy got to his feet, nearly stumbling over himself as he rubbed his jaw.

"Son, if you don't know the answer to that, I ain't gonna tell you," Will said with a shake of his head that indicated disbelief.

"Yah, vot did you hit the boy for?" All of a sudden, the farmer was butting in, trying to take control of the situation. After all, this was his property.

Buckskin appeared in the doorway to the barn, taking in the scene before him. He too gave a shake of his head as he took in Bill Hardy standing there.

"You know, boy, that's the second time I've seen you make a jackass out of yourself," the mountain man said. To the farmer, he said, "That's why he hit him, mister. This fool's making a profession outta acting like a jackass."

"I don't like this, not von bit." The farmer, a scowl on his face, seemed determined to have a say in what was going on.

"Believe me, I don't either, mister. I don't either. But don't get mad at me," Will said evenly.

"And vy shouldn't I?"

"Hell," Will said, tossing a thumb over his shoulder at the back door entrance to the barn, "them two pilgrims are riding *your* horses!"

CHAPTER

★ 11 ★

My horses!" The farmer literally spit the words out, a slow stream of saliva dribbling down the side of his lips as he said the words. With a fast glance at the silver star on Will Carston's chest, he said the only thing that came to mind. "Go! Go! Go, Lawman, whoever you are." He made shooing motions with his hands as he spoke. "You must catch them, catch my horses. Bring my horses back. Now. You must go now!"

Technically, Will Carston had accomplished his mission for he had the rest of Emmett's horses back. Back in Curious was the third horse that Emmett had lost to these horse thieves, the one that belonged to the wounded man who had ended up with the broken neck. Will recalled that before he'd left Curious early that morning, he'd made a deal with the owner of the hotel to keep an eye on the horse until he returned to pick it up on his way back to Twin Rifles. So technically he had done what he was supposed to, meaning that he could refuse help to this farmer. However, Will also knew that you simply didn't do that out here in this land. If someone was in need of help and you had the capability to assist them, why, most often you helped them out. It was no more than the way of things, for you knew that they would likely do the same for you if the need arose. So no matter what his options might have been, Will Carston knew as soon as the man asked him that he would ride out after Kyle Garret. Besides, he was a federal lawman and this man was entitled to protection under the same laws as Emmett back in Twin Rifles—or anyone else, for that matter. Of course, there was also the fact that twice now he had Kyle Garret in his grasp and twice the man had managed to escape. Will Carston didn't like that one bit.

"Round up a couple of hackamores," Will said to the farmer. "Give 'em to Hardy there."

"Me?" Hardy said skeptically.

"Yeah, you," Will replied. Eying the lad sharply, he continued. "It appears to me I'm better off having you around where I can keep an eye on you rather than having you spring surprises on me like you been doing. Like it or not, you're going with us."

"And how do you figure that?" The boy's tone was suddenly filled with defiance. "I'm free, white and—"

"And in my custody, is what you are, Hardy," Will said with a note of finality. "And that, son, is that."

"Stepped in it again, boy," Buckskin said with a wry grin. "Why, at the rate you're a-going, you may never get turned loose of the Marshal here."

Will went outside and took his horse to a watering trough, giving him one last drink before he left. He knew it would be a long afternoon.

"I think I hit one of 'em," he said when Buckskin came over to him.

"Ain't no thinking about it, hoss," the mountain man said with a nod. "I seen red on one of their shirts and I don't believe they got it from painting this here barn. Besides, that's why I shot the other one."

"As soon as Hardy gets those hackamores on Emmett's horses, you two play catch up with me," Will said, mounting his horse.

"Why not just leave Hardy and the horses here? Seems to me he'd be more a burden than anything else riding with us."

Will shook his head. "Like I said, I want him where I can keep an eye on him. The horses too. Remember, Buckskin, we're dealing with horse thieves. Don't want to make their life any easier than I have to."

Buckskin shrugged. "You're the boss." He slapped Will's horse on the rump and said, "Have at 'em, Ranger."

Will followed Garret most of the afternoon without catching up to him. But then, the mounts these horse thieves were riding were fresh ones and likely running fast and hard. Will's horse, on the other hand, had been riding all day so far, with only half an hour's rest at the German farmer's place.

The only thing that made the trail any easier to follow was the occasional drop of blood along the trail. Wherever Buckskin had hit Garret's riding pard, it was a part of the body that drew a lot of blood, that was for sure. In fact, as much blood as Will had seen by the time he stopped tracking that day, he was sure the horse thieves wouldn't gain on them that night, for they would be in need of rest, especially the wounded man. The lawman had been wounded before and knew from experience what that was like.

Young Bill Hardy and Buckskin caught up with Will about an hour before sundown. It wasn't long afterward that they decided to make camp for the day, for the sun wouldn't be up much longer. The old mountain man had spotted game in the area and immediately took to tracking it down as his two partners made camp and put the coffee pot on the fire. Will built a fire and measured out coffee beans to boil while Hardy tended to the horses.

"You want to tell me why it is you're tracking me and doing your best to get in my way, son?" Will asked Hardy when he'd returned from watering the horses.

"You sure are touchy, Marshal."

"Well, you've got to admit, son, I've every right in the world to be short-fused. Hell, you ain't been doing nothing but getting in my way since I left Twin Rifles. And I thought I'd left you there when I left you there." By the time he'd finished speaking, Will's face had turned into a deep seated frown that was anything but friendly.

Hardy squatted down, then crossed his legs and took a seat opposite Will and the fire. "It's like I said, Marshal, I just wanted to help you out."

Will's frown didn't change. "Even after I told you I didn't need or want your help?"

Hardy shrugged helplessly. "I reckon." His voice had lowered considerably. Humbled, you might say.

Will waited for what must have been two or three minutes for Hardy to answer, to explain himself further. But the young gambler didn't. So when the coffee began to boil, Will quickly grabbed the hot handle and pulled it from the fire, leaving it sit at the edge of the flames. He poured his own cup, then realized he didn't have one for Hardy.

"You got a cup to drink from?" he asked the lad.

Apparently, Hardy was now feeling so badly about what had happened that day that he didn't even pay attention to much more than what Will said. Which was when Hardy said, "In my saddlebags, behind you, Marshal. You'll find a cup somewhere in there."

Will half turned and spotted Hardy's saddle and saddlebags. He leaned over and, with one hand, rummaged through one of the saddlebags, finding the cup Hardy had said was there. But as he pulled out the cup, he also pulled out a piece of paper that had been folded over many times and fell to the ground beside the saddle. From what he could see of the big, bold print inside, Will thought he recognized it as a wanted poster of some sort. He placed the half folded paper in his lap as he poured Bill Hardy a cup of coffee and handed it to him. The boy didn't seem to be paying any attention to him, wrapped up in his own thoughts.

It didn't seem anywhere close to ordinary that a young gambler like Bill Hardy would have a wanted poster in his possession, which was what prompted Will to take a gander at it in the first place. And it turned out it was a good thing he did. The poster read:

WANTED—DEAD OR ALIVE
KYLE GARRET
$250.00
FOR THE MURDER OF
FREDERICK LAWRENCE

"Where'd you get that?" It was Hardy, and he was suddenly full of questions.

"From your saddlebags. It fell out when I pulled out your cup," Will admitted. He'd never found much use in lying about things. What was it Mama had said? Honesty was the best policy, or something like that? Still, he felt a little embarrassed about being called out like this. He tried to chuckle, as though making light of the situation, as he said, "You know how it is, a lawman sees a wanted poster, he's always wondering if it's one he ain't seen before."

"You shouldn't have done that," Hardy said, his voice showing a flash of anger now.

"That may be, son, but what I'm thinking now is how it is you come on carrying a wanted poster about in your saddlebags," Will said in an even tone. "Most drifters I know, they travel mighty light. Wouldn't carry any more than they had to where they stow their gear. Gamblers, hell, most of them travel even lighter. So what I have to ask myself is, what are you doing with this wanted poster of Kyle Garret?" He gently waved the poster before him, making sure the lad saw it again.

"That's none of your business."

"Well, whether you like it or not, I'm making it my business, son," Will replied. "Think about it a minute. I'm sitting here across the fire from a young man who's all but personally helped Kyle Garret get away from the long arm of the law twice. And here I go and find a wanted poster on the very man I'm chasing in your saddlebags. That just don't make one whole helluva lot of sense, if you set your mind to it, does it?"

If Will was expecting some sort of cooperation from

his companion, he wasn't getting it. "Like I said, it's none of your business." He's a bullheaded sort, Will thought to himself as the lad spoke. In fact, Hardy was beginning to remind Will of his oldest son, Chance.

"And like I said, I'm making it my business." It was almost like two bulls butting heads on the field of battle. And just like those two bulls doing battle, one was young and the other was old. "Now, you'd better start answering my questions or I'm gonna get mad, and I guarantee you'll regret that."

Bill Hardy rubbed his jaw, remembering the wallop the lawman had given him earlier in the day. He still felt a certain amount of pain, couldn't quite move it around freely like he should be able to do. He was silent for a moment before looking Will Carston straight in the eye as he said, "You'd better pour us another cup of coffee, Marshal. I've got a story for you to listen to."

Will poured them both more of the black stuff and sat back, slowly sipping his coffee as Bill Hardy spoke.

It all started five years ago, when his parents had died in a Sioux Indian attack up in what was then the Nebraska Territory, and he was all of fourteen years old. "Somewhere between hay and grass," was how he described it. They had lived on a farm, and when the house was burned to the ground in the Indian raid, the Lawrences, his next-door neighbors—if you could call next door four miles away—had taken him in as one of their own. They had a son of their own about Bill's age and the two got along real well.

Young Hardy had lived with them for the better part of four years and they were enjoyable ones. The two boys had become fast friends. But it was a year ago that the two had been riding the range by themselves, looking for stray steers and any mavericks in the area . . . it was that day that changed Bill Hardy's life forever.

"He came riding up, bold as day," Hardy said now, hate filling both his voice and the look about him. "Kyle Garret and close to half a dozen others. Killed Fred before he even went for his gun, Garret did. Then his men beat the hell outta me, gathered what cattle we had, and rode out of there."

"And Fred was the Frederick Lawrence on this poster?" Will asked. It didn't take long to fill in the blanks.

Hardy nodded silently, his face still that of a hate-filled man.

"I left the Lawrence place the afternoon they buried Fred. Been tracking Kyle Garret all over the Nations up north and in parts of Kansas," Hardy said in a calmer voice. "Stealing and killing seems to be his way of life, so it wasn't hard keeping track of his whereabouts. It surprised me he hadn't been to Twin Rifles before I'd arrived."

"Kept alive all that time by playing cards, I suppose?"

"That's right. Sometimes it amazes me how good I've gotten at the pasteboards in one year's time."

"Then what you're out for is revenge more than anything else," Will said, more as a statement than a question.

"More or less. Oh, I could use the two-hundred-fifty, mind you, but it don't make much difference to me. Hell, it could be twenty-five-*thousand* and it wouldn't mean no more than the two-fifty on that reward poster now," Bill Hardy said. When he added, "All I want is to kill that son of a bitch Garret and do it in person," Will knew the boy meant it with all his heart.

"I believe you," Will said, and he too meant every word he said.

"I reckon me walking in on you was my biggest mistake since setting out after Garret," Hardy said. This time he inched a smile up at the corners of his mouth, as though trying to see something humorous in the whole situation despite the fact that he truly hated the man they were after. "Believe me, I wasn't trying to make your job harder or see if I could get Garret free so I could light into him myself."

"If you say so." Will found himself believing the young gambler and his tale of woe. It wouldn't be the first time a man had set out after someone with revenge in his heart and as much ammunition as he could carry. Take Cora's death. She'd been killed by a band of raiding Comancheros. Her death wound up being avenged by Will and his two sons, who had become killing mean by the time they tracked down those birds. Killed every one of them dirty Comancheros too, they had. Yes, Will knew exactly how young Hardy felt.

"Well, now, ain't this something," Buckskin said as he entered camp, a prairie chicken and a rabbit in his grasp, his Hawken rifle setting in the crook of his arm. "You two having you a social tea, are you?"

"Just talking over a few things, hoss," Will said in an even tone.

"Finally decided to git friendly with one another, huh?" the mountain man said as he squatted and set to plucking the prairie chicken.

"Not really," Bill Hardy said. It was obvious that the old man was getting nosy. It was even more obvious that the young gambler wasn't too keen on discussing the matter.

"Ain't got so much as a morsel of rumor I could ponder on tonight?" Buckskin gave them both his toothiest smile.

Bill Hardy's face turned to stone as he glared at the old mountain man and, with an air of finality, said, "Old man, *it ain't none of your goddamn business.*"

It was then that Will Carston decided that even if the lad didn't have an awful lot of tact, he was definitely long on guts. And out here that counted for something.

CHAPTER

★ 12 ★

Rachel almost dropped the coffee pot she was in the process of taking from the stove top when she heard the thunderous crash of dishes in the dining room. Without a second thought, she quickly set the coffee pot back down on the stove and rushed through the kitchen doors to the long community table.

"My God, mother, what happened!" she exclaimed as she entered the room.

It was the end of the noon meal, with only a handful of patrons still seated at the community table, finishing their meals. Apparently, the crash of the dishes had surprised them as much as it had Rachel, for they all seemed to be staring at Margaret, who had dropped them.

"What happened, mother?" Rachel said again. She

had received no response from her mother the first time she'd asked that question, and she got none now. A frown formed on her face as she took in her mother, who was simply standing there and staring down at the floor in a daze. She couldn't recall ever seeing her mother in this condition. Rachel placed a gentle arm around Margaret's shoulder and began to guide her away, toward the kitchen area. "Come, mother. I think you need to take a bit of rest." Over her shoulder, she said to the customers, "I'm sorry about the accident. Please forgive us."

"Accident, my foot!" proclaimed a drummer who had an arrogant look about him. His words proved the look to be a fitting one. "Damn clumsy, what that woman done. Got that damned soup all over my shoe!"

Dallas Bodeen was seated across from him, both men seated on the end of the table nearest the kitchen entrance. It was when Dallas saw the anger quickly take form in Rachel's eyes as she glared over her shoulder at the man that he decided to take a hand in the matter. He reached across the table and took hold of the drummer's wrist, pinning it to the table and making the man immobile.

"Don't you worry, Miss Rachel," he said with a smile. "You go right ahead and take care of Miss Margaret. I'll tend to this flannelmouth for you." As Rachel helped her mother toward the kitchen area, Dallas had the notion she felt a mite relieved at his words.

"See here, you old bag of—" the drummer started to say. But Dallas applied pressure to the inside of the man's wrist, the pain cutting the man's words short.

"No, you listen, you pompous ass," he growled, leaning across the table as he spoke. "You shut your mouth or I'll break your goddamn wrist, understand?" When it didn't look as though the drummer believed Dallas, the old mountain man dug a thumb nail a bit deeper into the inside of the man's wrist.

"Yes, yes!" the man said in a pleading tone. "I understand, I understand! Now, please let me go. You're hurting me." He almost seemed on the verge of tears.

The drummer's wrist still firmly in his grasp, Dallas Bodeen stood up, reached for the bowler he was sure belonged to the man, plunked it on his head and guided him toward the front door. Outside, he pinned the man against the wall not far from the Ferris House entrance.

"I don't know how much longer you're gonna be in this town, mister, but I'm gonna give you some mighty solid advice," Dallas said, the growl still present in his voice. Along with it was a deep frown atop smoldering eyes that were indeed dangerous. "What that woman did in there was make a pure and simple mistake. Got it?"

"Yes, sir," the man said, all traces of bravado now gone. "I understand."

"And I don't want to hear you so much as *think* about making some cuss word remark to either one of those Ferris women while you're in town. We don't talk to the women that way hereabouts. You got that?"

The drummer, now nervous, nodded his head up and down in a swift manner, eager to please. Words seemed to fail him now.

" 'Cause ary I even suspicion that evil little mind of yours is thinking of speaking foul to Miss Margaret, why, you're gonna have whatever it is you've been eating on your shoes instead of just soup."

Dallas had the man backed up against the wall in

more ways than one and both men knew it. With that in mind, the mountain man playfully began to straighten the man's tie and dust off his suit with a mythical brush. When he next looked at the man, the salesman's face was still ashen in hue.

"Say, mister, you're looking mighty peaked," he said with a grin that soon grew wide. "I reckon you oughtta make tracks over to Ernie Johnson's Saloon and have you a drink."

"That sounds like an excellent idea," the man quickly said and was soon out of the mountain man's grasp and glad of it, making his way across the dusty streets of Twin Rifles, likely counting the hours instead of the days until the next stagecoach to his destination would be coming through town.

"And mister . . ." Dallas yelled after the man.

It took all the energy in his being to stop, but the drummer did just that in the middle of the street. "Sir?" he said over his shoulder.

"I'd change my attitude before I come in here next. Miss Margaret, she don't serve jackasses."

"Yes, sir."

There was only one man still seated at the community table when Dallas stepped back inside the Ferris House. Another drifter he'd shared his meals with the past few days. Regret, he thought his name was. He noticed the man was staring at him, smiling the kind of smile that was reminiscent of the cat who ate the bird. He didn't like it.

"Well, what the hell are you smiling at?" Dallas said, a bit of the same growl he had used on the drummer still evident in his voice.

"You," the man replied, still grinning. "And the way you handled that man."

"Well, mind your own business. Wasn't nothing

funny about it," Dallas said as he passed by, heading toward the kitchen and the Ferris women.

There was something about that man that just rubbed him the wrong way, Dallas thought as he entered the kitchen.

"What in blazes went on out there?" Rachel asked before Dallas could fire his own questions at her. "Mother's never done this before."

Dallas could only shrug, as confused as Rachel about the whole incident. "Beats me," he said. "She was bringing a bowl of soup out to the table when all of a sudden she froze solid as them Shinin' Mountains. It was as if she seen something far off, something that scared the bejesus outta her. That was when she dropped that bowl and just stood there like you found her. Couldn't move ary she wanted to, I don't believe."

Dallas and his description had Rachel rattled now, not knowing what to do, for her mother now sat in a hard-backed wooden chair, as motionless as she'd first seen her. And she still had that far-away gaze, the look Dallas had so accurately described as scaring "the bejesus outta her."

"Want me to get Doc Riley?" he asked, seeing the distressed look on her face.

"No." Rachel shook her head back and forth, in two quick movements. "I'm not sure mother would want that," she replied without hesitation. "You know how proud she is. She wouldn't want something like this to get out to anyone."

"Not even Will?"

"Especially Will."

"Lordy, girl, what is it you figure to do to make her snap out of it?" For all of his years of experience, Dallas Bodeen seemed momentarily to be stumped.

"I don't know, Dallas." All Rachel could do was stare at the sad sight of her mother, who seemed to be able to do nothing more than just sit there in a daze.

Dallas frowned and scratched the back of his head, as though the process would help him conjure up an answer to this problem. After a few minutes, he raised an eyebrow, an idea forming in his mind.

"I could try something, but she ain't gonna like it, Miss Rachel, not one bit," he said almost shyly.

"Oh?" For the life of her, Rachel couldn't imagine what the old man was talking about. "Your version of castor oil, I take it. Oh, well, if it'll work . . ."

"Guaranteed," he said with a nod. "On the other hand, I reckon it's what I heard Doc Riley refer to one time as shock treatment. You know, like throwing a bucket of water on a man who's lost his consciousness."

"I suppose if it will get her out of this stupor . . ." Rachel said with a shrug of indifference.

"Then here goes," Dallas said.

He moved around to the front of Margaret and knelt down on one knee. You'd have thought he was going to propose to her by the position he took. He looked up at Rachel, who was somewhat confused by what he was doing, slowly shook his head and took a deep breath. Then, ever so gently, he placed his hands on either side of Margaret's face, leaned forward and kissed her.

Dallas was right about everything. That one brief kiss brought Margaret Ferris out of her stupor. And she hated it. In fact, the whole process seemed to give her renewed strength for she immediately pushed Dallas away from her. And push hard, she did. She pushed him away so hard that he went sprawling on his back, sliding into a leg of the oven not far away. Quickly, he rolled away from the hot foundation.

"Get away from me, you dirty old man!" she all but yelled at him. She then ran her forearm across her mouth as gruffly as any mountain man might have, wiping any slobber he might have left on her lips . . . and gave a good healthy spit to the side.

Despite the fact that he was feeling some pain in his back, Dallas managed a smile for Rachel. With a chuckle, he said, "Told you, it works every time."

With a flabbergasted look about her, Rachel replied, "And I can see how."

"Why in the devil did you do that, Dallas Bodeen?" a now fiery Margaret Ferris said, the authority in her voice now at its fullest.

But Dallas was a quick thinker. "Why, to bring you back to your natural self, woman," he said in defense of his actions. Cocking a bold eye at Margaret, he added, "Part of which is a mean-spirited woman who it turns out can spit near as good as me." By the time he'd finished speaking, he was on his feet and looking down on the older Ferris woman.

Like many a redhead, Margaret Ferris was born with a temper, and it showed now. Her face seemed to screw up for a moment as she glared at Dallas. "Listen to me, you old piece of buzzard bait, you ever do that again to me and I swear you'll know what a gelded steer feels like."

From the time Dallas had kissed her, Margaret had been full of fire. However, it all seemed to go out of her now as she was suddenly quiet, her mind drifting back to what had happened out in the dining room. Her lower lip began to tremble and she soon had the look of a scared rabbit about her. Without a word, she gave one quick look to both Rachel and Dallas, then darted from the room, out the back door.

"I don't know what she's making brazen remarks like that for," Dallas said in awe.

"Why do you say that?" Rachel asked, still looking after her mother and her quick exit.

"Why shoot, girl, these past few years, I ain't all that sure I'd know what to do with a woman even if I caught up with one," he said in a lowered tone. The words he spoke were only a half-truth, for he'd said them partly to get Rachel's mind off her mother, although he seriously doubted that would be at all successful.

When Rachel bolted for the door, Dallas grabbed her by the arm and held her still. "But I've got to go to her," she said to him, pleading.

"No. You get this kitchen in order, girl. What you got is another meal coming up later today," Dallas said. Releasing the grip on her arm, he added, "Way I see it, she's a whole bunch mixed up right now. I reckon she might as well take her mean and hate out on the likes of me more than you."

He didn't hear Rachel say a weak "Thanks" as he barged through the door and went after Margaret.

He found her just out back, where the chopped deadwood was kept and stored for the many meals she and her daughter cooked. At first she didn't see him standing there in the doorway. It was then Dallas took in the beauty of this woman Will Carston had grown so fond of lately. Pushing forty from the north side and still had her good looks. You didn't find that in an awful lot of the women who'd survived life on this frontier. He would have concentrated on it more, were it not for the fact that she was crying. And when he saw that, he muttered something unspeakable under his breath. He never had been too good at handling a woman when she had turned loose the waterworks.

"I can see why Will's taken with you, Miss Margaret," he said as he walked down the few steps to the ground and sauntered over to her.

"Oh, pshaw," she said with a sniffle. "I've a good mind that my looks is what got me into this fix in the first place."

"Ma'am?" With that one sentence, she had thoroughly confused the old mountain man.

"Oh, never mind. It's none of your business, anyway," she said. Magically, her lace doily had appeared and she'd dabbed at her eyes and nose with it ever since she'd begun crying. Dallas made a mental note to have his big red kerchief ready to hand to her in about ten minutes if she kept on crying the way she was. If there was one thing he'd found out about women, it was that they could cry quicker—and more—than any flash flood he'd ever seen in his born days.

"Now, ma'am, I tend to differ with you on that," Dallas said. "You see, I dealt me a hand in this game when I led that foulmouthed drummer outside after you had your accident back there." Even though she wasn't looking at him, he found himself tossing a thumb over his shoulder at the Ferris House, which now stood to his rear. "Ary you don't mind saying so, I'd like to hear first hand what it is that's got you so upset, Miss Margaret."

Slowly, Margaret turned around to face Dallas. What she saw through her tears wasn't the gruff looking mountain man who so frequently took his meals at her table. Instead, what she saw was a man who had a gentle, although unshaven, face. And although he seemed to have trouble getting the words out properly, she was sure he was sincere in his efforts to make her feel better. Besides, at the moment he seemed to be the only one other than Rachel who was willing to listen to her sad tale.

"I wasn't being clumsy, like the drummer said," she said, wiping under her nose.

"Here," Dallas said and produced a big, red bandana he carried around in his back pocket. It was wrinkled and well used, a faded blood red to be sure, but he'd found that it served its purpose throughout the years. Hell, this wouldn't be the only woman who had shed a few tears into it. Not on your life, it wouldn't.

"Thank you," Margaret said and used the kerchief to dab at the side of her eyes.

Dallas desperately wanted to know what it was that was bothering this redheaded beauty, but he let her have her few minutes to gain some composure before she got to talking to him again.

"As I say, I wasn't being clumsy," she continued. "I'm afraid it was the look on the face of our Mr. Regret that caused me to drop that bowl of soup."

"That drifter that spends all his time in the shade?" Dallas said. When Margaret silently nodded, he added, "Never did like fancy dressers like him. Spend too much of their time doing nothing and acting like they got something."

"Yes. I think I know what you mean."

"But what was it about him that got you so upset?" he asked, a slight frown on his forehead. "Now, I know I ain't been here all that long, ma'am, but I'd never gauge you to be a woman short on words or character, especially as many times as you've cussed out the Carston men and me."

Although he was looking for a response to his

attempted humor, Margaret didn't give him one. Instead, she began to take on that horrified look Dallas had seen on her before, the look she'd worn in the dining room after dropping the soup. When she spoke, the words were dull and lifeless.

"It was the look I saw on his face, on Rance's face," she said. Her eyes seemed to be fixed straight ahead, perhaps at what she was imagining to be his face, Ransome Regret's face. "It was the same look I'd seen on his face the last time I saw him, so long ago."

"Oh? And what happened then?"

That was when Margaret told Dallas the same story she had recently told her daughter for the first time. About her romance with Abel and Ransome Regret's love for her and his jealousy and how he'd almost raped her. She told him every bit of it, and when she was finished she looked physically and mentally drained.

"Oh, Dallas," she said, breaking out in tears again, "what am I going to do? I'm so afraid of him and what he'll do to me. I feel like it's all my fault."

Facing her, Dallas took hold of her shoulders and looked her right in the eye, as he said, "Now, you just hush that kind of talk, Miss Margaret. Hell, I don't see how a woman as fine looking as you could bring anything but beauty into this world." He gave her a short smile and a wink. "Have you taken a look at Rachel lately? Why, she's the spitting image of her mother."

Dallas never did know if he was the cause of it or not, but all Margaret Ferris did then was cry more, cry harder. She simply stood there looking so helpless and so like a little child rather than the full-grown woman she was. It baffled him something fierce.

"It's gonna be fine, darlin'," he said as he slowly

took her in his arms, wrapping his huge arms around her and hugging her to him. "Everything's gonna be just fine." But all she did was bury her face in his chest and cry.

He didn't know if it was the right thing to do, take her in his arms like that. Hell, it was all he could think to do at the time!

It was all he needed to do.

CHAPTER

★ 13 ★

Buckskin turned out to be as good as he claimed when it came to tracking.

The next morning Will awoke to a cold chill in the air and knew it was more than a bit unusual for this time of year. He fed the fire some kindling and got it going again, preparing a pot of coffee afterwards. He was the first one up, but it wasn't long before Bill Hardy and Buckskin began to stir in their blankets.

"Kind of cold, ain't it?" Hardy commented as he stretched, still half asleep and shivering. Like many a man, the first thing he did was plunk on his hat and shake out his boots, just in case some kind of smaller wildlife had decided it needed shelter during the time he was sleeping. Being clad from top to bottom in buckskin, the old mountain man had only to reach for his beaver hat. He'd grown accustomed to wearing his moccasins and leggings day and night.

"Smell that air?" Buckskin said as he arose and began to roll his blankets.

"Yeah. Ary my nose ain't lost its scent, I've a notion we'll be running into rain not too far along in the day," Will said, feeding the fire more deadwood.

A couple of thick slices of bacon and a biscuit were all they had for the morning meal, along with a cup or two of coffee to wash it down. A body had to have the coffee this early in the morning, no matter what. Each man had learned to risk burning the tips of his fingers to sop the biscuit in some of the remaining grease once the bacon was done. To a fancy connoisseur this might not have seemed like much, but the grease tended to add a bit of bulk to a meal as skimpy as this one.

By daybreak they had broken camp and were saddled to ride. No one had to say anything, for each knew that with the prospect of rain ahead during the day they would have to cover as much ground as possible in tracking Kyle Garret. Each man had dug out a slicker before breaking camp, and it was now draped over his saddle and ready for use when the storm broke.

They rode steady for those first couple of hours, although never really pushing their mounts to a gallop as they continued to track the horse thieves. The sun had just barely broken through the horizon that morning and was soon beaten back by a group of dark clouds that bullied their way toward them more and more as the morning wore on.

"Say, just how come you're on this trek, Buckskin?"

Hardy asked, when they stopped to give their horses a breather about mid-morning.

"Why, cain't you tell by looking at me, I'm an experienced man in tracking?" the old man said, taken aback at the young man's words.

Will chuckled. "Don't let him pull you in too much, kid. Hell, I can track as good as or better than this old reprobate," he said with a wink and a nod. To Buckskin, he cocked a feisty eye and said, "You ain't the only one who rode with Bridger and Broken Hand Fitzpatrick and old Jed Smith and their ilk, you know."

It was the truth and Buckskin knew it. He just didn't like it. With a growl, he muttered, "I maintain I come to track these varmints. Yes, sir."

But Will wasn't having any of it today. "Horse apples, you old scoundrel," he said defiantly to the old-timer. "Hardy, he's got the same curiosity in him you do. Come along for the same reason too, as far as I'm concerned."

"What's that?"

"Why, to get in my way, of course!"

Hardy laughed at Will's words, knowing they were said in only half-seriousness. Buckskin, on the other hand, looked as though he'd had his feelings hurt and remained silent for the next ten minutes. Either that or he was awful good at looking like a man who's just been kicked in the elsewheres. A short time later, they mounted up and readied to continue their adventure in tracking Kyle Garret.

"There!" he said atop his mount, pointing to a thunder cloud that looked more than a bit ominous on the distant horizon. "That's why I'm here. I'll show you pups, I will. You just wait'll that storm strikes and

105

you find they ain't no more tracks to follow. By God, I'll show you!"

"Stubborn old bastard, ain't he?" Hardy commented as Buckskin quickly galloped away.

Will chuckled to himself. "Almost reminds me of me."

Bill Hardy silently nodded his understanding, then the two of them rode off to catch up with the old mountain man.

They only got another hour's worth of tracking in before the storm hit. The three of them had their slickers on as soon as the first few drops of rain fell, but Will wasn't about to stop and wait for the storm to pass. He urged his companions on, following Garret's tracks until the rain had totally washed them away. But before the tracks were gone, he had made a mental note as to the direction in which they were headed.

The rain came down hard and steady for a good twenty minutes, Will thought. Not in sheets, the way he'd seen it do before sometimes, but in big brazen drops that went plop-plop-plop and made themselves noticeable. As it was they were stuck out in the open and had to brave the elements for that twenty minutes before the rain let up. All Will could think of during that time was how nice it would be if they could find even a small cave opening somewhere in those mountains off in the distance by the end of day.

"So much for my monthly bath," Buckskin said once the rain had stopped.

"Let's find us some high ground and see can we get us a fire going," Will suggested.

"Wet as it is, I'll admit that some hot coffee would taste mighty good about now," Hardy said.

"You fellas take my share of this deadwood and see can you put it to good use," the old-timer said and untied a bundle which had set atop his saddlebags all morning, tossing it to Bill Hardy. Before they had broken camp that morning, they had gathered up as much dry wood as possible and split it up between the three of them. Wrapping each bundle in a piece of leather that had been coated with bear grease to water proof it, they each tied an equal share behind their saddles. They had known the storm was heading their way—and knew the need for dry firewood would still exist at the end of the day. The odds of finding any after a good drenching in this land were next to nothing, and all three knew that too.

"What are you gonna do?" Hardy asked the old-timer.

"I'm gonna see just how far this storm rained. Mebbe pick up some tracks a ways out, ary I find a place it didn't rain like a cow on a flat rock with no control of its bladder," Buckskin said with a knowing smile. "Besides, I got a notion old Garret and his friend had to stop during that downpour too, just like us."

Will and young Hardy shook themselves out of their slickers and set about building a fire and making a pot of hot coffee while the old mountain man rode off in the direction the trail was headed.

"Old Buckskin seems to think he knows a right smart amount about tracking this Kyle Garret," Bill Hardy said in an offhand manner, once the coffee was made and he and Will were sharing a cup.

"Yeah, old-timers like that tend to act like they've been everywhere and done everything," Will said with a smile.

"Sort of like you?" Hardy smiled too.

For a moment Will had a mock look of hurt on his face. "Please, son, I'm not *that* old."

Buckskin was gone for close to an hour, by Will's calculation. When he rode back into camp, he looked as though both he and his mount had done a good deal of riding.

"Find anything?" Will asked, handing the man a cup of hot coffee and a cold biscuit.

Buckskin took his beaver hat off and slapped it against his leg, as though from force of habit. Before answering, he took a big bite of the biscuit and swallowed half his cup of coffee.

"Nope. Thought I had something for a bit, but it turned out to be deer tracks," he said and took another bite of biscuit and drink of coffee. "Getting old in my old age, I reckon."

"Just remember, you said it, I didn't," Hardy said with a facial expression close to a sneer.

By the time they saddled to ride, the sun had broken through the clouds and it looked as though the afternoon would bring much better weather than they had seen that morning. Much drier weather, at least.

Buckskin insisted on taking the lead now, claiming his expertise as a tracker would keep them on the trail to the horse thieves. Will grudgingly let the old-timer have his way, knowing that he would keep track himself of just what trail they were following. After all, he knew as well as the old mountain man what direction they would have to lead off in. Once they got past wherever it was Buckskin had tracked to, it would be anyone's guess where Kyle Garret and his friend were.

"Here's how we're gonna do this, gents," Buckskin said before they rode out. "Youngster, I want you to head off fifty, mebbe seventy-five yards off to my right," he said to Bill Hardy.

"What then?"

"Then you face directly west toward them mountains and look for signs of this Garret fella. Understand?"

Hardy nodded.

To Will, Buckskin said, "Marshal, I'd like you to wander off to my left about the same distance and do the same thing."

"And you?" Will asked.

"While you boys are riding ahead, I'm gonna be riding back and forth in a zig-zag between the two of you. Way I see it, we oughtta pick up their trail a mite easier that way. Cover more ground, this chile thinks."

Will hadn't thought of it before, but the man's idea seemed to make sense. Rather than the three of them following one trail, they would be covering a larger expanse of the trail. And considering how predictable Kyle Garret and his partner were, the odds seemed to favor the pair heading west toward the mountains more than in any other direction.

"Sounds like a right fine idea," Will said.

"Why, of course it is! Now git to it, lads. And give holler ary you find something," Buckskin said as Will and Hardy headed for their positions.

They spent most of the afternoon tracking the horse thieves in this manner, the sun warming their bodies and drying them off as the afternoon wore on and the mountain range got closer and closer. The rain, apparently, had covered a good share of this land, for they rode all afternoon without coming across so much as a trace of any other horse tracks.

It was later in the afternoon that Will began to think more of Margaret Ferris than the outlaws they were chasing. Although he wouldn't admit it to either of the men with him, Will had had Margaret on his mind a good deal of late. She'd been a part of his dreams at night and was constantly on his mind during the day, which was perhaps why he tried so hard to keep busy at something, in this case tracking a horse thief. For the life of him, he couldn't forget the look in her eye that day he'd left, couldn't forget how persistent she had been with him that day. He would have to talk to her about their relationship when he got back, try and make her understand the fact that, although he liked her immensely, he didn't know if he was ready to marry again.

After all, what good would it do to marry again? He'd spent over thirty years with Cora, only to wind up losing her to some crazed Comancheros who had raped and killed her. He would always remember the grief he'd felt over losing that woman, the pain he had gone through upon her death. And the vengeful satisfaction he had felt when he and his boys had caught up with the sons of bitches and killed near all of them. He knew all too well that he didn't want to go through that kind of pain again. Nor did he wish to subject a woman like Margaret Ferris, who had lost her own husband of twenty-some years, to that kind of pain should he lose his own life while carrying out some law enforcement job. It just wasn't fair.

He was half reading what little signs were before him and half thinking of how he would explain all of this to Margaret when he returned, when a shot rang out, bringing him very much back to the reality of the day.

He knew in an instant that it came from the mountain range. It took a second longer to see that Buckskin was still in his saddle, while Hardy's horse was empty. He wheeled his horse to the right and kicked at his flanks, urging the animal on as he headed for Bill Hardy's position. As he rode, he pulled his Remington from its holster, keeping it at the ready, and gave those mountains another quick glimpse.

He saw nothing. Not even the smoke from another rifle shot. It had to be a rifle shot, for it not only sounded like one, but they were still a good distance too far off to be hit by anything less effective than a rifle of some sort.

A second shot rang out as he arrived at Hardy and his mount. Will thought it dug into Hardy's saddle, for the horse jerked, then jumped from the shock. Buckskin pulled his own horse to a halt near Hardy about the same time.

"I seen the smoke," he said and slid down off his mount, bringing his Hawken rifle to his shoulder and firing at the mountains. They all waited a moment before hearing the ricochet of his .58 caliber bullet careening off the walls of the ravine he'd fired into. It didn't seem likely that he'd hit anyone, but the return fire suddenly put a cease to their own fire.

"You all right, son?" Will asked, fully taking in Bill Hardy for the first time since he'd reined in his horse.

"Whoever it is, ain't too awful good a shot," Hardy said and looked down at the top of his right shoulder, where a bullet had grazed him. "Reckon I'll live."

"Bad shot or a warning," Buckskin said by way of observation.

Will nodded. "That's what I'm thinking too."

Buckskin patched up Hardy's arm while Will kept an eye on the mountains, looking for movement so he'd know where to head. This was an awful big mountain range. By the time Buckskin and Hardy were ready to move on, Will had decided that whoever had done that shooting had either moved mighty quick or was feeling confident about crawling around like a snail up there, for he surely didn't see anything.

"Not a damn thing," he said when they asked what kind of movement there was in the mountains.

"Doesn't look like a helluva lot of daylight left," Hardy said when they mounted up. "Will, you mentioned something about finding a cave earlier. I say we concentrate on finding something up in those mountains to give us and our horses some shelter in case it starts raining again. What do you think?"

Both Will and Buckskin knew that there were at least two more hours of daylight left, enough time to do a good deal of tracking if you were of a mind to. But in a way Hardy was right, for tracking a body in mountains, any kind of mountains, was next to impossible. Besides, if that was Kyle Garret and his compatriot up there, they had almost caught up with the two. And unless they went awful slow—to avoid making a lot of noise and drawing attention to themselves—they weren't going anywhere too soon. So looking for a cave to put up in for the night wasn't all that bad an idea, if you thought of it.

"Yeah."

"Sure."

So they headed for the mountain range and searched out a cave to provide shelter for them. And as they rode toward the mountains late that afternoon, the mountain man and the lawman gave each other one more furtive look. Their eyes said what each of them knew in their heart.

Although Bill Hardy may have been slightly wounded that afternoon, he was now showing all the signs of being scared to death.

CHAPTER

★ 14 ★

While Buckskin, Will Carston and young Hardy were searching out a vacant cave to spend the night in, Dallas Bodeen sat at the community table in the Ferris House and ate his supper meal. But he too was doing some searching out.

Margaret had calmed down considerably since telling him her tail of woe about Ransome Regret and her youth. She had even gone on to confide in Dallas that afternoon he had held her in his arms. What she had said didn't seem all that much of a bother to Dallas, but it sure did seem to trouble Miss Margaret. What she was afraid of most—other than Ransome Regret himself—was the idea that Will would find out what had happened once Regret had come to Twin Rifles. If he were to find out what Regret's intentions were, why, Will would track the man down and kill him for sure.

"It's that serious?" Dallas had asked, a note of concern in his voice.

Margaret Ferris had blushed as she muttered, "Yes." What she had meant, of course, was the situation between Regret and Will Carston would be a serious one. But what Dallas took her answer to mean was that the relationship between she and Will, his best friend, was indeed as serious as he had thought all along.

With that in mind, the old mountain man had begun searching out ways to teach this Regret character a lesson. There were plenty of ways this could be done, but nothing an old fur trapper like himself could get away with within the city limits of Twin Rifles. As much as this drifter had hurt and scared Miss Margaret, the first thing that came to Dallas's mind was making the son of a bitch undress bare-ass naked and staking him to the ground while he stripped one inch pieces of his flesh from his worthless carcass. The Blackfeet had always been good at that. Finally, it crossed his mind that, as well liked as Margaret Ferris was in this town, why, he could likely get a mite of help in figuring something out. Which was when he headed for Ernie Johnson's Saloon.

Now, as he finished his supper, Dallas found himself casually engaged in conversation with Ransome Regret, who was seated right across the table from him.

"Mighty fine, Miss Margaret," he said, pushing a near spotless plate away from him, patting his belly with his other hand. "Yes, ma'am, you set a fine table."

"Well, thank you, Dallas," Margaret said with a pleasant smile and leaned across the table to pick up his empty plates. "Are you sure you wouldn't like another piece of apple pie?" She was being inordinately considerate to the old-timer, when you took into account her usual lack of kind words for him. Several of the other guests that night could only exchange confused glances with one another at her change of attitude. For the most part, they would likely have agreed with her about Dallas and his lack of manners.

"No ma'am," Dallas smiled, a satisfied look about him. "Two pieces is my limit tonight." Dallas himself was surprised when Margaret had offered him a second helping of the tender roast beef she was serving that night. Along with the offering of food, he was also astonished at the composure this woman had tonight. Compared to what had happened earlier in the day, why, she was a rock of strength now. And it purely amazed him, it did.

"Excuse me, Mr. Regret," Margaret said with a smile as smooth as her hands as she rubbed against the drifter, having retrieved Dallas's plates. Without a doubt, Regret was enjoying every second of it.

"That's quite all right, ma'am," he said with a polite smile that Dallas expected to turn into a leer any time now. And when he did . . .

But Margaret was gone before anything could take place and both men watched her leave the area as she headed for the kitchen, her arms stacked high with dirty plates and silverware.

"She's quite a lady, isn't she?" Regret said, the politeness in his smile now replaced by a look that could only be taken as a leer.

But Dallas counted to ten before he said anything,

knowing that to do otherwise would spoil it all. After all, what was it that Mama claimed old Thomas Jefferson had said: "When angry, count ten before you speak; if very angry, a hundred." The only reason Dallas didn't count to one hundred was because he didn't think he had the time.

"Oh, yes, she's quite the lady, friend," was all he finally said, doing his damnedest to hide his true feelings.

When Margaret was out of sight, Regret took one last sip of his coffee and got up from the table. "Well, if you'll excuse me, sir, I'll go back to finishing my book . . . or what I can with the light that is left of the day."

"I used to read a lot in my youth," Dallas said, also rising from the table. He had to think quick, for it was imperative that he keep a conversation going with this man. It was all part of the plan.

"Is that so?"

"Oh, yeah, up in the Shinin' Mountains, back in the fur-trading days. Taught myself how to read one winter," he added with a faint smile. It was a part of his life story that was known but to a handful of men, the trouble he'd had with reading.

Regret was taken by surprise at Dallas's words. "You taught *yourself?*" he said in a tone filled with amazement. "I find that hard to believe."

Dallas shrugged, a bit embarrassed at what he was saying. After all, this was all part of the plan, keeping a conversation going with Regret. "Didn't have much in the way of schooling back where I come from."

"Then, how did you teach yourself?" The man now seemed to be fascinated by the subject at hand.

"Actually, we had one of these nature fellas along with us that fall. Called himself a natural scientist, I do believe. Right smart fella, he was. Edicated and all, you know."

"And he was the one who taught you to read?"

"In a roundabout way, I reckon you could say that," Dallas said, continuing his story. "Days got so long and cold in the winter that a lot of us would take along books to read. Why, some had that Shakespeare fella to read. *Clark's Commentaries on the Bible.* Titles I forgot long ago."

Regret nodded. "Clark is an interesting read, if you're a religious sort." It was obvious that whatever else he might be, Ransome Regret had a great deal of knowledge of books and reading.

"What happened was, old Nuttall—that was his name, Thomas Nuttall—he'd read those big books and I'd kind of memorize 'em as he read. Had a memory near as good as Old Gabe, I did. Then, when he was finished, I'd go back and pick up the book and turn to the chapter he was reading from and piece those words and passages together. Picked up a heap of words that way."

"Remarkable. And do you read now?"

Again Dallas shrugged. "Lost the urge, I reckon. Or maybe it's because they's a lot more to do out here than just read, pleasurable as that may be. Besides, this town ain't all that well known for having a whole passel of books on hand."

Regret made his way into the drawing room, to the chair he had occupied nearly all day every day since arriving in town. He picked up a book he'd apparently placed there, as though to assure his seat while he left to eat dinner. The marker in the book indicated he was nearly through with the big leather bound volume. "I've only got a few minutes of reading left before I'm done with this," he said as he took his seat.

"I'll give it to you when I'm through, but only under one condition."

"And what's that?"

"That you read it sometime soon."

Dallas grinned broadly. "Mister, you've got a done deal."

Dallas waited patiently for the half hour it took Regret to finish his book. He didn't want to seem overly eager, but as soon as the drifter closed the text, Dallas almost rushed to his side.

"Say, I been thinking, hoss," he said, knowing that it pained him to call a man "hoss" who was nowhere close to being a friend, even if he was making him a present of a book.

"What's that, friend?"

"Ary you got some free time the rest of this evening, I'd like to buy you a drink. You know, show you the appreciation I should for giving me that tome of yours."

Regret seemed genuinely pleased, smiled. "Well, thank you, sir."

"Dallas. You can call me Dallas."

With a pleasant enough smile, Regret snatched up his hat and placed it squarely on his head as he said, "Well, then Dallas, let's go have a drink."

Dallas squinted down at the book as Regret headed for the door. Unless his eyes were failing him, the title was *"Great Expectations."* The author was Charles Dickens.

"It's quite a good book, actually," Regret said, seeing him from the doorway. "Long, but overall quite good."

"I'll keep that in mind," Dallas said as they left.

* * *

Ernie Johnson's Saloon didn't have the crowd it usually did, which was fine with Dallas. For what he had in mind, he didn't need that many participants, not if it was to come off right.

Dallas and Regret each had a drink, exchanging small talk. It was while they were on their second drink that Emmett approached them.

"Say, Dallas, how's your luck running?"

Surprised, Dallas gave an indifferent shrug. "Pretty good, I reckon. Old Regret here, he just give me a book by that fancy writer, Dickens his name is."

"Sounds good," Emmett said, giving the mountain man a firm slap on the shoulder. "How'd you like to join us in a poker game? Pardee and me figured we'd find us a couple more players. Two handed poker ain't much of a challenge, you know."

"Sure. I reckon I could give my luck a try," Dallas said in a friendly manner. He tossed off his drink and was about to turn to go when he remembered Regret, still standing there at the bar. "Say, Emmett, what about Regret here? Four's better'n three, you know. His money any good?"

Emmett gave the man a broad grin. "Long as it ain't Confederate, I reckon it is."

"What do you say?" Dallas asked his drinking friend. "Want to play a hand or two?"

"Why not?" Regret finished his drink and followed Dallas and Emmett to a table in the rear of the saloon, where Pardee Taylor was shuffling a deck of cards.

"Evening, gents," Pardee said and continued to shuffle the deck of pasteboards.

The table was located in the rear of the saloon, offering even less light than could be seen with at the bar. As the players took their seats, Emmett lighted a coal lamp attached to the wall. The flame sputtered before coming to life and shedding the necessary light needed to play in this corner of the room.

"There, that oughtta help," Emmett said as he took his seat.

Dallas noticed that Regret had taken a chair with his back against the wall, the way a superstitious gambler might. It immediately crossed his mind that if this man had been concentrating so hard on trying to scare Miss Margaret, why, he'd likely spend a good deal of his time right here at this table while he was in town. His kind usually did.

He also took in Pardee Taylor, who had dressed in what must have been his good clothes and his Sunday-go-to-meeting jacket. It was likely as formal as you'd ever see the man get.

"You ever played Old Cat?" Pardee said, trying to act as professional as possible at the role he was now playing.

Ransome Regret looked a bit confused for a moment before politely saying, "No, I'm afraid not. But if you explain it, I'm sure I'll catch on after a hand or two."

Pardee explained that Old Cat was a local version of five-card draw poker that was played by the folks of Twin Rifles. Deuces, aces and sixes were wild.

"Are you sure it's wise to have that many wild cards?" Regret asked when Pardee was through talking. "It would seem to me that an awful lot of high hands could be held in this game. That would run up the stakes considerably, wouldn't it?"

"Look at it this way, sport," Emmett said to Regret. "It ain't high stakes so much as a test of seeing how long a man is on guts."

Regret chuckled. "Or how foolish."

The look on Emmett's face didn't change one whit. "There's that, too. Yeah."

For Regret's benefit, they played a couple of exhibition hands to give him an idea of what to expect when they started playing with real money. From the look on Regret's face, he was at first surprised at the cards he drew, then thinking the devious thoughts of greed that most folks only saw on their banker's face.

The first two hands dealt out, Regret bid small amounts, dropping out of the first hand, even though he had an ace with a pair of jacks. In a game like this, he must have figured that three of a kind wasn't going to win much and he was right. Dallas laid down a pair of fours and a six and a deuce, claiming four fours.

The second hand dealt, Regret again bid small amounts to the kitty, but actually managed to win the hand when Dallas and Emmett folded and Pardee turned out to be bluffing.

There was only ten dollars in the pot, but the fact that he had won seemed to boost Regret's confidence and the man played a more daring game on the third hand dealt. Again he won, this time a pot of fifteen dollars.

"Looks like you're picking this game up real quick, sport," Emmett, who was down three dollars, said. "You sure you ain't played this before?"

A good deal of pride showed in Regret's face as he shrugged and said, "No. Honestly. Granted, I've played some games that were similar to this, but nothing as wild as Old Cat."

As Pardee dealt the fourth hand, Dallas was sure his plan was going as scheduled. As for Regret, he drew two cards and held a hand of five sevens, betting heavily into the pot. When Dallas and Emmett dropped out, there was only Pardee Taylor left holding a hand, and Regret must have thought the man was again bluffing as he matched Regret in his betting. There was at least a hundred dollars in the pot when Regret laid down his hand, smiling from ear to ear.

"Five sevens," he said and swept an arm out and around the money on the table, ready to rake it in to his side of the table. But before he could rake in the pot, Pardee laid down his hand.

"Not so fast, friend," he said with a grin that seemed twice as wide as Regret's. "I've got an Old Cat." The cards snapped down on the table, revealing two aces, two sixes, and one deuce.

"A what?" Regret said in disbelief.

"An Old Cat," Pardee said. "Any time you get a hand full of wild cards, why, that's an Old Cat."

"And?" Regret was suddenly acting obstinate, and with good cause.

Pardee chuckled to himself. "Mister, you got to learn how to read signs," he said and pointed to the one on the wall directly in back of Ransome Regret. It read: AN OLD CAT BEATS ANYTHING.

"What!" Regret said, nearly choking on his own words. "You didn't tell me that! You didn't say a damn thing about that." His face turned into a harsh frown as he glared at Pardee. "Say, what are you trying to do, cheat me?"

"No, honest! I must've forgot, Mr. Regret," Pardee said in an apologetic manner.

"I think you're right, Pardee," Dallas said, as though suddenly realizing the dealer's error. "Why shoot, boy, your memory's getting worse than mine, and I'm old as dirt."

"Tell you what, sport," Emmett said to Regret, "why don't we all just take back what we kicked in the pot and call this hand one for experience, huh?"

"Well . . ." Regret took a minute to consider the ex-cavalryman's words before agreeing.

"This way you can't say nobody's cheating you," Emmett added as an afterthought.

"You want someone else to deal?" Pardee asked Regret.

Regret started to reach for the deck then stopped and said, "No, you go ahead." So far the hands he had gotten had been pretty good ones. Could it be fate or just the way the dealer tossed out the cards? Apparently, Regret was going to put his faith in Pardee Taylor and his dealing expertise.

Emmett won the next hand, taking in about ten dollars and making up for the five dollars he had been down. A family man couldn't afford to lose much at gambling, especially with a wife and two kids to feed.

Regret won the next hand and got some of his gambling confidence back. It was during the next hand that Regret's eyes nearly dropped out of his head. And it wasn't at the cards he drew. No, sir. It was at the cards he had been dealt! He bet heavily again, tossing in twenty-dollar gold pieces, followed by forty dollars in greenback currency into the pot. Once again Emmett and Dallas folded early, leaving only Regret and Pardee to duel it out.

"An Old Cat!" he all but yelled as he laid down an ace, three sixes and a deuce. "Beat you! Got you this time," he added and began raking in the money in the pot, which came to well over a hundred dollars.

"Not hardly," Pardee said in a low, angry tone, laying down a deuce, a ten and three treys.

Regret stopped in mid-motion, an incredulous look about him. "What did you say?"

"I said not hardly," Pardee repeated in that same angry tone.

"But that's impossible. I've got an Old Cat. I've—"

"Mister, I don't mind giving you a break when I'm the one who made the mistake, but I ain't about to be responsible for everything you do," Pardee said. Dallas thought he was trying real hard to sound like Chance Carston, whom he consorted with quite a bit between jobs. "Like I said, read the sign."

Ransome Regret hastily turned around and took in the sign to his direct rear, the one saying that an Old Cat beat anything.

"Yes, I see it. So what? The pot is mine, I win the hand," he said, his confidence boosted.

"No, not that one. *That one,*" Pardee said and pointed with his arm at the second sign on the wall, located about three feet above the first one. Just as Dallas had figured, Regret was so caught up in playing this wild card game that he'd paid attention to only the one sign, the one directly to his rear. But it was that second sign that took the wind out of his sails. It read: AN OLD CAT IS ONLY GOOD ONCE A NIGHT.

It was then that Ransome Regret knew that he had been snookered. Or maybe it was seeing the look on Pardee Taylor's face as he raked in the pot to his side of the table.

"You son of a bitch," Regret grumbled as he reached inside his coat pocket and produced a four barrel .41 caliber Derringer. He was cocking it and aiming it right for Pardee when he stopped what he was doing. He stopped because he heard another pistol being cocked off to his side. He froze stiff as a rock when he turned his head slightly and saw the business end of a Colt's Army Model not three inches from his face.

"Here now, that'll be enough of that foolishness," Joshua, Will Carston's deputy, said, holding the six-gun as steady as could be. He also had an all business look about him, so Regret laid the Derringer down on the table. "You just hand that toy of your'n over to me and let's us talk about what's the matter here afore we go to shooting off more'n our mouths." Silently, Regret did as he was told.

"But I was cheated, Deputy," he said in protest and proceeded to explain the game being played and what had transpired, placing special emphasis on the signs behind him and the part they played in his being cheated.

After hearing Pardee tell his side of the story, Joshua put away his Colt's and shook his head.

"I gotta tell you, mister, you're treadin' on mighty thin ice here," he began, trying to imagine how Will Carston would handle this. "Old Cat, why, that's the most favoritest game in this here town, it is. Why, women even got to playing it at them hen parties they hold. Way I figure it, children'll likely be picking up on it next. Playing during recess at school, can you imagine?"

"But the signs. Surely they can't be legal. They're just signs, put up to dupe whatever sucker is drawn into the game," Regret said, acting as though he were sure he had the answer to this dilemma.

"Oh, no. Them's legal as can be. Put up by the town council theyselves, they was," Joshua said with a straight face. "Mayor got so many complaints about people cheating at the game, he went and passed two ordinances. One of 'em states that an Old Cat beats anything. And the second, why, it says—"

"An Old Cat is only good once a night," Regret said, already knowing what it was he would hear. "I should have known."

"Say, tell me something, son," Joshua said, scratching his head, as though in afterthought. "You can read, can't you?"

"Well, of course, I can, you fool!" Obviously Regret was offended by the remark, particularly by a man he likely figured to be some sort of buffoon.

"Oh, he can read fine, Joshua," Dallas said. "Why, he just give me a copy of a book by that Dickens fella."

"That being the case, I'd say you lost yourself a hand of poker, Mr. Regret," Joshua said to the man. "A hand of Old Cat, at that."

"So that's it, huh? You're all in on it." Regret stood up and grabbed his hat, planted it firmly on his head. He then held out his hand, as though expecting the deputy marshal to hand his pocket pistol back to him.

"I'm afraid you also lost the use of your toy gun while you're in this town, friend," Joshua said in an even tone and stuffed the Derringer into his vest pocket. "You see me afore your stage leaves town and I'll turn this back over to you."

Regret was making his way to the batwings when Joshua called his name out.

"What is it?" a perturbed Regret snapped at him.

"You know, I read something writ by one of them back East writer fellas oncet."

"Do tell."

"Something about it mattered not whether you win or lose, but how you played the game, I believe it was."

"And?" Regret's patience was wearing thinner each second.

"Well, I thought about that some and I do believe that fella was a mite wrong in what he said."

"Just what is your point, Deputy?"

"Why you, Mr. Regret. You," Joshua said. "You're a perfect example of what I'm thinking on."

"And that is?"

"Why, I reckon it don't matter whether you win or lose . . . until you lose," Joshua said with the hint of a knowing smile on his lips.

Dallas wasn't sure whether it was the words or the look on Joshua's face that made Regret storm out the door the way he did. Just the same, he had a good feeling about him when he saw the man leave in that condition.

"Looks like that young Bill Hardy taught you well, Pardee," Dallas said, giving the man a hearty slap on the back.

"Yeah, he sure does know how to double deal, that Hardy fella," Pardee said, apparently amazed he had dealt as good as he did.

"You do a pretty good job yourself, Pardee," Dallas said with a grin.

Dallas had a drink or two with his comrades, all of whom were having a laugh at what they pulled off with Ransome Regret, before heading back to the Ferris House.

When he walked in, he gave a brief look at the spot on which he'd left the copy of Dickens before leaving for the saloon with Regret.

The book was gone.

"Goddamn Indian giver," Dallas muttered to himself as he went to his room.

CHAPTER
★ 15 ★

They had been fortunate enough to find some dry wood in the cave and used it to make their fire that night. What was left of their own firewood they would save until the following morning. By then, they reasoned, the storm would have passed and they would be able to find more deadwood to use at their camp later that day.

With game scarce since the breaking of the storm, they used some of the provisions Will and Buckskin had each packed away before setting out on the trail for Kyle Garret.

"Reckon I'll have to do the hunting tomorrow," Bill Hardy said as he finished his meal for the night and refilled his coffee cup.

"And why's that, young 'un?" Buckskin asked with a raised eyebrow.

Hardy turned a sudden red at his neckline, obviously embarrassed about whatever it was that was bothering him. "Well, all I've been doing is eating while you fellas have done the providing. It is your grub we're eating."

"Don't worry about it, son," Will said, dismissing the lad's worries with a wave of the hand. "It ain't nothing but a matter of survival out here. Hell, I ain't about to turn a man away from my camp just because he ain't brought the necessary provisions with him. That's pure foolishness. You ought to know that."

"That's right, sonny," Buckskin said as an afterthought. "Why, ary you're getting a case of the guilts about pulling your weight on this trek, you just make sure we're well supplied with firewood from here on out and we'll call it square. What do you say?"

Hardy let out a sigh of relief. He was silent, apparently in thought, for a moment as he took a sip of coffee. Then, with a slight frown, he took in Buckskin again. "You sure you don't want me to do some hunting for us?"

Buckskin let out a hearty laugh, the kind that comes straight from a man's belly. "No thanks, sonny. I ain't seen a gambler yet who could handle more'n a palm gun with any accuracy. No, sir, you just stick to gathering firewood."

Will smiled to himself, sure now that young Bill Hardy wouldn't find the gathering of deadwood to be all that useful a task after hearing what the mountain man had just said. Will had known for many a year now that the use of words could do much more to belittle a man than looking down the barrel of any type of weapon, no matter what the size of the bore. Of course, that also meant a man had to use his head before he used his mouth too, which was likely why so many of these youngsters were always getting into trouble of some sort. Take that young Clay Allison fellow he'd met a while back . . . But that was a whole 'nother canyon.

Apparently, at one time or another, this cave had been used as a hideaway by someone else. Like anyone else with good sense on this frontier, whoever it was had laid in some extra firewood before leaving. It was this firewood they had used for their evening fire that night. And after they had finished with that meal, Buckskin had done some scrounging about and come on a pile of old buffalo robes farther back in the cave.

"Here's what'll keep you warm tonight, boys," he said as he tossed a robe on the ground next to Will and one next to Hardy. He also dropped one on his own side of the fire. All three of them knew that the fire would go out long before the middle of the night arrived, leaving the cave a cold and dank place to be, especially after the rain they had experienced that afternoon. The lawman and the gambler mumbled a thank you to Buckskin.

The old mountain man pulled out his possibles bag and dug in it for his cleaning materials, setting to cleaning his Hawken rifle before the light of the fire was completely gone. Will and Hardy had given their own weapons a once over as the coffee was boiling earlier.

Feeling an urge to stretch his legs, Will headed for the mouth of the cave and, discovering the rain had ceased and the skies had cleared a bit, ventured out into the fresh air of the night. With only a few minutes of light left, he decided to spend the time watching the beauty of nature as its view slowly disappeared for the day.

He was soon joined by young Hardy, who stood there only long enough to take in the sight of the sunset before remembering what the old mountain man had charged him with.

"Reckon I'd better gather up some wood before there's no light left at all," he said in a matter-of-fact way. He then proceeded to make his way through some of the still wet brush in the surrounding area and pick up pieces he judged small enough to dry within a day or so. He knew that the next visitor to this cave would be in need of the same amount of supplies as he and his friends had used.

"Wonder what range of mountains this is?" Hardy asked once he'd completed his task and taken up a position next to Will. The sun was nearly out of sight now, the young gambler hardly able to make out Will Carston's profile in the approaching darkness.

"Couldn't tell you for sure," was Will's reply, still gazing out at the disappearing ball of fire that had been the sun. It almost seemed as though he were going to get in every last sight of it, no matter what the man next to him wanted to discuss.

"They look big enough to be a part of the Rockies," Hardy said, a touch of awe in his voice.

"Some would say so," Will shrugged. "Never had much truck with the mountains of west Texas. Most of my traipsing around in the Rockies was done up Colorado and Wyoming and Montana way. At least, that's what they call 'em now. Back then they was just the Shinin' Mountains, all the way up north to all the way down south. And then some."

Bill Hardy smiled at the older lawman's remembrances. "That's what I hear."

There were many small mountain ranges in the extreme western portion of Texas, although not many had the height or breadth Will Carston had recalled the Central Rockies as having. The further one investigated these ranges, the more he would find mountain tops of several thousand feet, many not unlike those found throughout the Central Rockies. It was just that old-timers like Will Carston could never get over the hugeness, the greatness of the mountain ranges they had known as the Rockies.

"I get the impression old Buckskin knows a whale of a lot about this Kyle Garret fella," Hardy said after a brief silence.

"Oh? I got the impression the old man was bragging more on his tracking skills than anything else," Will said. "Or am I missing something here?" Every once in a while Will had to ask himself if he was getting old. In the back of his mind, he knew this was inevitably true. However, like many a man of his age, he liked to put it off for as long as possible.

"No, it ain't that," Hardy said, as though a bit confused about it all. "I mean, he don't do a lot of bragging on Garret at all. Why, he's the quietest mountain man I've ever met. Not that I've met a lot of 'em, you understand."

"I understand."

"It's just that . . . well, I got a feeling about him."

"A feeling?" Will found himself suddenly curious about this young man's views. "And what's that?"

"I'm thinking he knows a lot more than he's letting on. He just seems too mysterious to me."

"I see."

When Will didn't say any more, the young gambler said he would be turning in shortly and disappeared back into the cave, leaving the lawman to his own thoughts.

In those few final moments before dusk totally consumed the night, Will Carston gave serious thought to what young Hardy had said about Buckskin. That he was an odd sort there was little doubt. Of that Will was sure. But what about this talk young Hardy had brought up about the old mountain man knowing Kyle Garret? How could he know Garret? Will had gotten the distinct notion that if anyone knew Kyle Garret well, it was Bill Hardy. After all, hadn't he been the one who had his heart set on avenging the death of his friend? It was a fact. So if anyone might have ulterior motives, Will was sure it would be Hardy rather than Buckskin.

On the other hand, the lad did bring up an interesting point. For a mountain man, Buckskin sure was a subdued fellow. Most of the men Will could remember carousing with were loud and boisterous types, the ones who were quiet only when they were certain there might be a Crow or a Blackfoot nearby. Of course, there had been the ones like Jedediah Smith, the quiet ones who hardly ever cursed or raised their voices in any matter. Now, those were the ones a body had to keep an eye out for, those were the dangerous ones. But from the few outbursts he had heard from Buckskin, Will doubted he was anything close to Jed Smith in his bearing.

He was about to turn back into the cave and retire for the night when it struck him. Had the old-timer, the old mountain man simply bragged about his tracking prowess, or had there been something else? Indeed there was. I must be getting old, Will thought to himself as he scratched his head in wonder. It was then he remembered that Buckskin had also made some forthright comment when he'd met him the morning he left Curious. And that comment had been about the old mountain man being able to lead Will straight to Kyle Garret. At first he'd taken it as nothing more than an idle boast by a man who was in all likelihood well past his prime as a mountain man or a tracker. Still, it got a man to thinking. Was it just a boast, or did old Buckskin really know how to lead Will straight to Kyle Garret? If he did, it could only be for one reason: He knew where Kyle Garret's hideout was.

All of which brought Will Carston to wondering the same thing the gambler Hardy had brought up earlier that night. Just how was it this Buckskin knew so much about Kyle Garret?

Buckskin had stood inside the mouth of the cave all the while the young gambler and the lawman had held their conversation, taking in every word of it. It wasn't that he was a gossip or anything, so much as he wanted to know what was being said about him.

It was when he heard Hardy say he was turning in that he scampered back to his buffalo robe and quickly wrapped himself up in it, pretending to be asleep. Apparently it worked, for he could hear young Hardy wrap himself up in his own robe, followed shortly by Will Carston when he turned in.

What the lawman and the gambler had been discussing about him seemed interesting indeed.

Yes, sir, real interesting.

CHAPTER
★ 16 ★

Some men have an inner mechanism that goes off as though it were an alarm clock built into their body. Will Carston was such a man, coming awake an hour before daylight. He built a fire and put the coffee on to boil before stepping outside the cave to take in the fiery red of the early morning sun as it broke through the eastern horizon. It wasn't long before he was joined by Hardy and the old mountain man, Buckskin.

"Quite a sight, ain't it?" Buckskin said to anyone who would listen.

"Almost as good as an evening sunset," Will replied. Hardy nodded agreement. After a good deal of silence, Will added, "The black stuff ought to be boiling by now," and headed back inside the cave to serve himself a cup of coffee.

Buckskin went through the same motions, as he began to fry up several slabs of bacon for the trio of men. When the fatback was ready, they ate their morning meal and prepared to move on as the sun rose in the sky.

The rain had stopped early the previous evening, a slight wind picking up during the night, a wind that seemed to dry much of the greenery in the area. They did their best to leave the cave as well supplied as they had found it for the next visitor who happened by, with plenty of near dry deadwood stacked for use.

"Where do you reckon they're at now, Kyle Garret and his friend?" Hardy asked as he tightened the cinch on his mount that morning.

"This chile's guessing they're either up the mountain or over the mountain, one," Buckskin said, a dead certainty in his tone. "Couldn't go round the mountain. That's a damn long trip."

"You're likely right, Buckskin," Will said. "They had to fight the storm the same as we did. Of course, it didn't rain last night, so they could have made their way over the mountain if getting away was on their mind."

Both the young gambler and the old mountain man agreed it was a possibility to consider as they moved out, Buckskin once again in the lead. This would have been fine were it not for the fact that both young Hardy and Will had their individual thoughts and suspicions about Buckskin on their minds.

Bill Hardy kept racking his brain for some sort of hidden information on Buckskin, trying to recall if he might have seen him in the crowd that had come to kill his friend that day a year ago. But he couldn't place him, for he didn't recollect a geezer like this old-timer in the pack of wolves Kyle Garret had been running with.

Will was thinking basically the same thing, with more emphasis placed on the statement Buckskin had made about being able to take Will straight to Garret and his hideout. In fact, the deputy United States Marshal was almost sure that if Garret—or Buckskin—was going to make a move against him and Hardy, it would likely have to be today. Rain storm or not, they were getting too close to the horse thief for Garret and his bunch not to make a move of some sort. After all, the odds of the man simply surrendering to Will out of the blue were next to nothing. Men like Kyle Garret didn't give up all that easy. Not on your life.

"Whew," Buckskin said, running a sleeve across his sweating brow about midday, when they pulled to a halt to rest their mounts. "It sure does want to heat up a mite." The sun had come out in full force by now, the three men finding a trickle of a stream of water with which to give their horses a drink and a breather.

The old mountain man was right about one thing. To go around the mountain would mean to travel one hellacious distance either north or south to the nearest pass. So the three had agreed early on to traverse over the mountain as best they could, Buckskin sure they would be able to catch up with Kyle Garret quicker this way. No one had argued, but the man was right, the sun had heated up quite a bit this morning.

"I can spell you for a while up front if you'd like," Will said as the mountain man refilled his canteen in the stream.

At first the old-timer appeared to be skeptical about the offer, but by the time they had tightened their cinches and were ready to ride again, he had grudging-

137

ly admitted to Will that it would be a bit of a relief not being in the direct sun all the time.

"I'll watch our backsides," he said when they mounted up. "You just keep an eye to your front, Marshal, and look for a ravine not far up ahead. We'll have to take it single file, but once we do, we'll be that much closer to these yahoos."

Will paid little attention to the remark, walking his horse slowly among the rocks as they headed toward what looked like the ravine the old man had been speaking of. Only once did he glance behind him at Bill Hardy, who had a somewhat worried look on his face. For a man who was so anxious to mete out revenge, the young gambler's face held a hint of the same fear Will thought he had seen on the lad the day before, when the outlaws had fired upon him from the mountain ridge. Will also remembered Buckskin's remark about a gambler not being able to use more than a palm gun effectively, and found himself doubting Bill Hardy's usefulness, at least, if the look on his face was any indicator of his true feelings. Will remembered riding with men like that before and it got to be a dangerous proposition. A man often found himself to be the only one who could defend himself, especially when he was counting on his riding pard to lend a hand—not to mention an extra gun.

They came on the ravine Buckskin had spoken of, and indeed it was a narrow piece of trail to travel. Single file was the only way it could be traversed, with barely enough room to turn a horse around should things go bad, Will thought.

And they did.

A shot rang out, ricocheting high against the ravine wall. But Will thought it strange when he heard it for none of them had been hit, and he knew good and well that Kyle Garret could knock any one of them out of their saddle if he'd a mind to. As he was pulling his Remington from its holster, he had the faint notion that it might be a warning shot instead.

He was right.

Snapping a shot off in the general direction he took the gunfire to be coming from, he wheeled his mount around, ready to beat a hasty retreat back where they had come from. It wasn't seeing that Bill Hardy had done that very same thing much faster than he had that surprised him when he'd turned his horse around. Nor was it the fleeting thought that Hardy was a coward, ready to run at the sound of gunshots. What it turned out to be was the same thing that had surprised the young gambler as he'd wheeled his own horse about.

Buckskin hadn't moved one bit. Instead, he had pulled his horse to the right, bringing it about so the off side of the horse was facing Hardy and Will. That in itself might not have been so hard to swallow, for it wouldn't be the first time an old codger like Buckskin had made a stand with nothing more than a Hawken rifle to do his shooting with.

What surprised them was the fact that the old mountain man had his Hawken rifle leveled right at them, a wicked grin now covering his face.

"That'll be far enough, boys," he said, the expression on his face not changing one bit. Then, to the lawman, he said, "Like you said, Marshal, it's all a matter of survival out here. Now, I'd appreciate it if you'd turn your hardware over to me and get your hands up."

Will Carston and Bill Hardy didn't have a choice.

CHAPTER

★ 17 ★

Well Garret, did I bring 'em to ya just like I said I would or what?" Buckskin said in a confident manner as he entered the horse thief's camp. As a precaution, he had had both Hardy and Carston dismount and walk their horses back through the ravine. No need in making it easier for them to escape, he'd reasoned to himself.

The ravine had gone on about fifty feet from where the old mountain man had drawn down on the gambler and the lawman, opening up onto a piece of flat land that might have been all of two hundred feet in circumference. Located within the mountain itself, the area was open to the sky and the elements of weather, be they fair or foul. There were no trees within sight, the walls nothing more than jagged rock, some areas rounded by the wearing away of the elements of nature. When you thought about it, the wearing away of this whole land—not to mention the men passing through it—was being left up to Mother and Father, Buckskin thought as he took in the features about him. Mother Nature and Father Time. The thought made him chuckle.

"Yeah, you done a good job, old man," Kyle Garret growled, his eyes drilling Will Carston and Bill Hardy with what could only be described as pure hatred. Especially young Bill Hardy.

"Then I'll take my fifty dollars and be gone," Buckskin said with a lopsided grin. When Garret shifted his gaze to the mountain man only briefly, Buckskin added, "You did say you'd give me fifty dollars ary I'd lead 'em right to you, ain't that a fact?"

The horse thief momentarily ignored the old-timer, his evil stare falling to Will Carston. "You're the son of a bitch that shot me, ain't you?" he said as he walked toward him, a half a dozen long steps being all he needed. It was plain to see that the bloodied kerchief wrapped around the horse thief's upper left arm was proof that he had indeed been shot.

Will Carston had never been one to sidestep trouble. Nor would he back away from it. He saw the angry outlaw ready to bring his fist down on him as he neared the lawman and quickly set his mind in motion. Buckskin had their guns, which left him with nearly nothing to defend himself with. However, he had learned long ago that there are weapons everywhere a body looks; the trouble was most people didn't realize it. He could also tell by the furious look on Garret's face that the man had only one thing in mind at the moment, and that was knocking Will Carston to the ground. With that in mind, Will made a vicious swing of the rein in his hand as the outlaw hit him. Garret hit hard, knocking Will to the ground with a hard right roundhouse punch.

"Damn you!" Will heard Garret say as he lay on the ground. He focused his eyes and saw that Kyle Garret hadn't been the only one to hit his mark. Will had swung the leather rein hard enough to leave a dark red gash on the outlaw's face even as he had been falling to the ground. "You'll pay for that, lawman," he added with a deep growl.

"Not if I can help it," was Will's reply as he staggered to his feet, still stunned from Garret's glancing blow.

"You ask me, you're the one who's got some paying to do, friend," Bill Hardy said boldly. It was a tone Will Carston had not expected to hear from the young gambler. And it turned out to be a mistake for the lad.

"We'll see about that," Garret said, still sounding as mean as he looked this close up. He only contemplated whether or not to hit the boy for a second, wasting no time in pulling his own six-gun out in the bat of an eye and aiming it right at Hardy, his arm extended to its fullest proportion. "I remember you too, you young whelp. You was there when I done in Lawrence, wasn't you?"

The young gambler seemed unafraid of the man, whether he was looking down the business end of a pistol or not. "You've got a good memory, Garret," he said in a steady voice, a voice that almost dared the outlaw to kill him then and there. It was almost as though Bill Hardy had gone from being a rambling young man to a full-grown man in a matter of a day or so, the way he was acting now. "But I still say you're the one who's gonna do the paying." Bold all over again.

Will was sure Garret would have killed him on the spot if one of Garret's henchmen hadn't come up behind Hardy and put the butt of his rifle into Hardy's side, just above the belt line. Hardy quickly fell to his knees then rolled over on his side, both hands grabbing for the pain that was already prevalent in his face. Brave or not, the young man was groaning in pain as he lay there, helpless. It was one thing you found out real quick like out here; pain didn't care whether you were the bravest man in the world or the worst coward that ever lived. When it struck, by God, you knew it!

"Thanks, Croft," Garret said to the big man who had felled the young gambler. "Find a spot against one of these walls and have some of the men posted as guards over these two after you tie 'em up." Kyle Garret holstered his pistol and rubbed his knuckles, which were still sore from hitting Will Carston so hard a blow across the jaw. Then he ran a hand across his left cheek, which was now bleeding, if only slightly, and let out a curse at the lawman as he was led away.

"Sure thing, boss," Croft replied and directed two men to get Hardy to his feet as he began to push Will Carston toward the wall he would be seated at.

"And Croft," Garret said as his henchman began walking away.

"Yeah."

"Get fifty dollars out of my saddlebags and give it to the old reprobate here," he said, jerking a thumb toward Buckskin. "The sooner he's gone, the better."

"Right boss."

Kyle Garret had never meant to become a horse thief or a man killer, he'd just sort of fallen into it. The war had come to an end and there were damn few jobs about, and he had been damned if he was going to beg for his supper . . . so he'd taken to stealing an occasional horse to provide his trading goods for a trade of food down the road. The trouble wasn't that he'd gotten good at it. Hell, he'd always been good at handling horses. The trouble was that he'd gotten to like it after about six months or so. Add to that the fact that there were still damn few jobs about and you had the makings for a career as a horse thief.

For the year or so that followed, Kyle Garret had made his way across the frontier, taking horses wherever he could find them. As he did so, he also found that there were more men like him than he had imagined. They were just as hungry and just as desperate as he was and were soon joining him in his forays into the dangerous world of horse stealing. At one point he had even given the seven or eight men who had ridden with him a name of their own, calling them "Garret's Guerrillas" in the manner of any one of a number of raider groups that served both sides during the War Between the States. But the name had never caught on, at least not yet.

However, Kyle Garret and his men did have a wanted poster or two out on them in the states and territories that ranged anywhere from Kansas and Nebraska out to Colorado. The only places of any worth they hadn't been yet were Texas and California, and they were working hard on Texas at the moment.

Kyle Garret had been at this vicarious trade for more than two years now, and he had killed his share of men to get the horses he had come by. And so far the killings had either been justifiable or there had been few if any witnesses to them. The only bur in his saddle now was in the form of the two yahoos Buckskin had brought into camp, the lawman and the

Hardy boy. As they passed through Curious, Garret had been approached by the old mountain man, who was cadging for drinks, and offered him a job. The job was to lead the man who was trailing him, Will Carston at the time, to his hideout up in the mountains.

"All I want to do is scare 'em, old-timer," he'd told Buckskin. "Get 'em off of my trail, convince 'em to turn back, if you get my drift. Hell, a couple of horses ain't worth getting killed over, is it?"

The old-timer had agreed to do the job, persuading Garret to buy him three more drinks before the horse thief left the saloon. But now that had all changed. He hadn't expected the lawman to come charging in on his game of billiards. Nor had he expected to encounter him in that old farmer's barn while they changed saddles and stole some fresh horses. But they had met and the encounters had been close both times, the lawman winging him in the arm the second time as they escaped. Running from the law was one thing, for Kyle Garret had been doing it the better part of two years now. But being shot at, why, a man could take that right personal, especially if he got hit in the shooting.

That knothead Hardy was no better. As far as Kyle Garret could remember, the lad was the only one who had ever witnessed a killing of his and lived on to tell about it. In fact, Hardy was likely responsible for the wanted poster they put out on him back up north for the killing of Frederick Lawrence, Hardy's friend. Obviously, the lad would have to be taken care of. It was when Garret felt a twitch in his left arm and had to move it, a procedure that brought great pain to him, that he decided that the lawman had to be dealt with too.

"Looks like you was awful rough on 'em, Mister Garret," Buckskin said as he stood there waiting for Croft to bring him his money. "I mean, you said you was gonna scare 'em a mite, but that was a fur piece you taken that scaring routine, wasn't it?"

Kyle Garret gently rubbed his wounded arm, giving the old-timer a loathsome look. "Who says I'm meaning to just scare 'em, old man?"

"Why—" Buckskin started to say in protest before stopping. "Oh, never mind. It don't make no difference."

"That's a wise choice of words, old man," was Garret's reply, to which Buckskin said nothing in return.

Then Croft appeared, fifty dollars in gold coin in his hand. Without a word, he dropped them into Buckskin's outstretched hand and turned away, as though ignoring him on purpose.

"Croft, how's our supply of ammunition?" Garret said as the two outlaws walked away.

"Pretty good, boss. Why?"

"Because tomorrow morning, I want you and the boys to do some target practicing," Garret said with a leer.

Croft didn't say a word, only gave a lopsided grin back to his commander.

Buckskin pretended to be engrossed in counting out his fifty dollars of gold. But just like always, he heard the conversation between Garret and Croft in its entirety.

"What do you think, Will?" Hardy asked, his hands tied behind him, just like the lawman's. "How we gonna get outta this mess?"

"I think it's a helluva time for you to start getting

friendly with me," Will said sharply. "There's a difference between being a flannelmouth and being flat out brave with your words, you know."

If Hardy could have raised his hands to fend off the lawman's words, he would have. Instead, he simply settled for, "All right, Marshal. I didn't mean nothing."

"As for getting out of here, well, young man, I'd pull out my prayer book if I were you and start reciting something useful instead of sitting here palavering with me like we were best friends." Will still had a noticeable sharpness to the tone of his voice, and it wasn't because his jawline was still aching. After all, no man appreciates putting his faith in another man —in this case Buckskin—and then being fed to the wolves like some chunk of meat. You just didn't do it out here, and Will Carston knew it all too well. But then, most of these opportunists didn't have much in the way of a code of honor, unless it was among themselves. And apparently Buckskin was definitely one of the bad guys in this game.

They sat there in the sun the rest of the afternoon, quiet for the most part, each man in his own thoughts. Will found himself wondering if he would ever get back to Twin Rifles to see Margaret Ferris, swearing to himself that if he was indeed fortunate enough to escape from these outlaws, he was going to give her a big kiss, no matter who was looking. Bill Hardy only had one thought on his mind, and that was how he could loose his bonds so he could find a way to kill Kyle Garret. That was, after all, what he had come this far for, wasn't it?

It wasn't until Garret and his gang had fed themselves that Buckskin carried over a couple of plates of beans for them.

"Garret says I can't untie you, so I reckon I'll have to spoon feed you boys," he said as he knelt down on one leg. "I hope you boys are big on beans 'cause that's about all these fellers has got. No biscuits, no meat. Why, it's a helluva way to run a railroad, ary you ask me."

"Ain't got much of a conscience, do you, Buckskin?" Will said as the mountain man fed Hardy.

The old man fed a couple more spoonfuls of beans to the young gambler before replying. "As a matter of fact, Marshal, I been having a case of the guilts for the past couple of hours, I have."

"Oh?" The words purely surprised Will. "I thought you'd be long gone by now."

"Well, Marshal, it's like this. I reckon I spent the better part of this afternoon getting to know how that Judas fella must have felt. Mind you, I got fifty pieces of gold and not thirty pieces of silver, but I swear the guilts is still the same."

"Sort of like love and hate, I reckon," Will said. "Ain't none of 'em changed much in the last couple thousand years."

"Ain't that the truth." Buckskin set down the empty plate and picked up a now lukewarm cup of coffee and gave Hardy several big gulps of it.

"Come to any conclusions, did you?" Will asked.

"Not for sure, Marshal. I reckon I'm still thinking on it a mite. I'll let you know ary I make a command decision like one of them fancy generals."

"I hope you do it soon," Hardy said as Buckskin began spooning beans into Will's mouth.

"Yeah, I reckon I had ought to," the old-timer said with a shake of his head. "Gonna have to be soon too."

"Oh?" Hardy perked up at this part of the conversation. "And how's that?"

"Oh, you ain't heard then, have you?"

Both Will and Hardy frowned. "Ain't heard what?" Will asked around a mouthful of beans.

"Why, I heard old Garret mention to his top man that his boys was gonna do some target practice tomorrow morning."

Hardy gave a worried look to Will, who returned the same.

"You've got it, boys. He didn't say so, but this chile's guessing you fellas are the targets."

CHAPTER
★ 18 ★

Herod Kelly had always preferred that you simply call him by his last name. After all, Kelly could be a first name as well as a last name and in this land there were stranger names to have, especially for an Irishman. He had been born to a mother who was more religious than anyone he'd ever met, to include his uncle, who was a priest and quite religious himself. He never did find out why his mother had named him Herod, but the name had been a thorn in his side ever since his youth. He still couldn't figure out why anyone would want to have a son named after the man who was a king in the time of Christ. Why, that was as bad as being named Judas, for God's sake! So when he'd left home at the age of fifteen he made a point of telling whomever he met that he answered to Kelly, not going into further discussion as to whether it was his first or last name.

A big brash man of forty years, he sported a beard that had touches of the red of his hair, along with continually graying whisker hairs. For the most part he tried to carry on a civil conversation with those who were his patrons. But don't cross him or what had once seemed like laughing green eyes would soon take on a foreboding look that you wanted nothing to do with. Herod Kelly, you see, could be hell on earth to someone who crossed him.

Like Will Carston, Kelly had fought in the Mexican War, although the two hadn't met until after the war, when Will was trying to interest people in settling down at a little town he and Abel Ferris had established down in Texas. Kelly had been working as a gunsmith near St. Louis when word of Will's adventure got around to him. The two had talked and Will had convinced Kelly to move to Twin Rifles. It was there that he established the store everyone in town knew as Kelly's Hardware. Along with furnishing the town's hardware supplies, Kelly also doubled as the gunsmith for anyone needing their weaponry repaired. If Chance Carston knew how to shoot it, more than likely Kelly knew how to repair it. In fact, both men had spent more than a few hours exchanging stories about weapons they had used, shot and mended in their lifetimes.

But this afternoon it was Joshua who was holding court with the big Irishman as the day slowly progressed. The deputy, a puzzled look about him, had brought in an old Remington he had found in the drawer of Will Carston's desk.

"I tell you, Kelly, I learnt all 'bout how to shoot these here pistolas and such back when I was a chile,"

Joshua said, glancing at the handgun he'd laid on Kelly's counter. "But truth to tell, why, they reminds me a whole lot of a woman's corset, they do."

Kelly raised a curious eyebrow at the lawman's words. He had yet to hear of a weapon that could be compared to a woman's corset. "Oh? And how's that?"

"Why, don't you see, Kelly, I never figured out how them dang fool corsets worked either!" Joshua said, a sincere but frustrated look about him.

"From what I understand, Joshua, you're better off not knowing," was Kelly's advice to him.

"I believe you."

"Now, what is it that's wrong with this piece?" Kelly was prone to calling just about any weapon he worked on a piece. Some military training is hard to die in a man.

"Well, I ain't for sure." Joshua scratched his head as he spoke, looking down at the six-gun in puzzlement. "Like I say, I found it in Will's drawer. Figured I'd clean her up and see ary that wouldn't get her in proud working order. You know, have it ready for Will oncet he returned, just in case he was to needing it."

Kelly picked up the Remington .44, which looked to be an exact duplicate of the one Will Carston wore at his side. "Pretty good job of cleaning. I'll say that." He inspected the barrel and cylinder of the weapon, then spun the cylinder and worked the cocking and hammer action several times. "Sear needs a mite of work, I'd say."

"Fine. You think I could mebbe pick it up in a day or so, ary you're not too awful busy, that is." Joshua never was much on asking people to do things for him, preferring to do it himself if it was at all possible. But the Remington he had just cleaned had him stumped as to how it worked and what it was that needed doing to it. Yes, sir, it purely did. "I know Will is gonna appreciate it."

"Well, you can tell Will he's gonna have to take better care of his six-guns than this," Kelly said with a sad shake of his head.

Joshua thanked the gunsmith profusely and turned to go, bumping into young Tommy Roth, a freckle-faced lad of twelve with a shock of blond hair falling down across his eyes.

"Whoa there, pard," Joshua saïd, grabbing the boy by the arms to steady him, hoping he didn't hit him too hard.

"Sorry, Mr. Holly," the lad said as the red crawled up his neck and into his face.

"Nonsense, son." Joshua had known a good deal of criticism in his own youth and often went out of his way to be nice to the younger generation of Twin Rifles. "Say, I'll bet they let school out early agin, din't they?"

"No," Tommy said with a smile. "I wish they would, though."

To Kelly, Joshua said, "Now back when I went to school, why, they had us sitting in that classroom until near dark."

"Really?" Tommy asked in astonishment.

"Don't listen to him, Tommy," Kelly chuckled. "If the truth were ever told, everyone would know that old Joshua never got past the fourth grade."

The deputy mumbled something in embarrassment as Tommy snickered at the gunsmith's words and the joke he was making.

"What was that, Deputy? What did you say?" Kelly said with as straight a face as possible.

"I said I knowed all they is to know 'bout the fourth

grade," Joshua said in his humblest manner. "Went through it three times, I did." By then the red had taken over his own face and it was he who was feeling embarrassed.

"What can I do for you, Tommy?" Kelly said, now focusing his attention on his new customer. "Your Mama needing something, is she?"

"No. Actually, I feel kinda strange being here like this, but he gave me all of a dollar to do it," the young man said.

"You running errands for someone these days?" Kelly asked, not sure what to expect for an answer.

Joshua was suddenly showing a professional curiosity about the conversation going on before him. "Say, just who is this he you're a-talking 'bout?" he asked in a very official manner.

"That fancy dresser over at Missus Ferris's boardinghouse," the lad said.

"Regret's his name, isn't it?" Joshua could feel his insides go sour at the mention of the man's name.

"Yeah, I reckon."

"And just what is it he's wanting you to do for all of a dollar, Tommy?" Kelly asked, the look on his face now as curious as that on the lawman's own face.

"He give me this," the boy said and dug down in his pocket, producing a twenty-dollar gold piece. "Said he wanted whatever kind of six-gun twenty dollars would buy in this town." The words brought the eyebrows up on both men, for although Kelly hadn't been there he had definitely heard about the ruckus the tinhorn had started over at Ernie Johnson's Saloon the other night. Joshua, on the other hand, knew all too well what was about to be transacted.

"Well now, Kelly, just what is it you could sell the

man for a solid twenty-dollar gold piece?" Joshua asked warily.

"Well . . . if you don't want me to sell him one, I won't, Joshua," Kelly said. "You know that."

"No, you go ahead and sell him what you like," the deputy said, his back-hills mind turning over with thoughts he dare not speak. "Last time I read that Constitution, why, they claimed this was a free country. Body oughtta be able to buy and sell whatever it is he likes, I say. No matter what shape it's in." These last words came out with particular attention as Joshua spoke them.

Kelly was not a slow learner by any means and soon sported a smile on his face as he gave the lawman a slow nod. "I've got just the gun for him," he said and pulled out an 1862 New Model Navy revolver in .36 caliber. "I'll have it ready for him in no time."

"Tell me something," Joshua said, taking Tommy aside while Kelly readied the Colt's revolver.

"Yes, sir."

"You're daddy ever hit your mama?"

A shocked look came over the boy. "No, sir! Pa says he'll kill the man who lays a hand on Ma."

"Well, that's good, Tommy. A man ought never to hit his woman," Joshua said with sincerity, as though he were teaching a Sunday school class. "Now, listen son, I'm gonna tell you something about this Regret feller that I don't want you to ever tell another living soul, you understand?"

"Yes, sir. I can keep a secret."

"Good." Joshua felt as though he had done his civic duty when he was through telling Tommy the story he would take with him to his grave.

It was about then that Kelly had the Navy revolver ready to take back to Ransome Regret.

CHAPTER

★ 19 ★

Say, did I hear you right, son?" Buckskin asked the big one known as Croft.

"What's that, old man?" Croft wasn't exactly the most likable man he'd ever met, but then, the old mountain man didn't figure on knowing him all that long anyway, so it didn't really matter, did it? Now if you had to winter with a man, why, that was a whole different situation. But if you knew that the likes of Will Carston and that Hardy boy were fixing to kill as many of these pilgrims as they could, well, he could manage to put up with Croft and his kind for a while longer, no matter how ugly he sounded when he talked.

"Why, I thought I heard you and your boss say you was gonna kill those two birds tomorrow morning,"

Buckskin said, yanking his thumb over his shoulder at the sight of Will and Hardy tied fast against the sheer rock wall.

"You got big ears, old man," Croft snarled at him. "Maybe too big for your own good."

"Listen, sonny, ary I didn't have ears as good as the ones I got, why, I'd never have lived as long as I did midst a land that had Blackfoot and Crow popping out at you from in back of every other tree. Yes, sir, that's a fact." Buckskin wrinkled his nose and gave a stiff nod to Croft, as though to tell him off in his own fashion.

"They something to you, are they?"

"Hell, no!" he yelled. Had to sound convincing when you talked to a man as thickheaded as this one, Buckskin thought. "Why, I led 'em here for the fifty dollars your boss said he'd shell out to me. Nothing more, nothing less." The mountain man gave a greedy smile to Croft and patted his pocket full of coins. "And it looks like I come out the better for dealing with a couple of lousy human hides, don't it?"

"Then what's it to you whether they live or die, old man?" Croft said, still snarling when he spoke.

Buckskin shrugged, giving the big man his best humbling look. "I reckon it's just that your boss told me he was gonna scare these boys up some. He didn't say nothing 'bout wanting 'em dead, you know."

"Well, it's gonna happen, old man, so you'd do well to shut up and mind your own business," Croft snapped at him.

Still acting humble, Buckskin said, "I'll keep that in mind, friend."

Croft gave him a pitiful degrading look, shook his head in disbelief, and walked away from Buckskin, surely having better things on his mind, the old mountain man thought. But as he watched him go, he knew that he'd gotten the answer to his question. One other thing was certain in Buckskin's mind too, as he watched the big man amble off. "I'm gonna kill that son of a bitch," he all but whispered to himself, as though swearing an oath to himself when he spoke.

He'd been in tight fixes before, this old reprobate, and somehow gotten out of enough of them to live to be about seventy-five years of age. But it had always been Indians and other trappers or those damned suppliers trying to take you for everything you had . . . it was them he'd always had his dealings with. Not a boxed in hole of sorts with only one way in and one way out. In more than a manner of speaking, this was a whole new canyon for Buckskin, an entirely different situation than he had ever been involved with before.

How was he going to get out of this fix? How was he going to get the marshal and the young snot-nosed gambler out of it with him? At first his mind went blank and he couldn't think of anything that would work. Walk up to them and ask them to surrender? I'm laughing! he thought to himself as he banished the thought from his mind. They were sure enough the enemy and had to be treated as such. Still, it had paid to be friendly to at least the chief honcho while he was still here. Being friendly, now there was an idea.

A half an hour later, just as the sun was about to set for the day, Buckskin had been to his horse and scrounged through his possibles bag, coming up with just the right thing for what he had in mind.

"Say, boys, what say we pass the jug a mite afore the day's all but gone for good?" he said as he produced a small jug for all to see. There were five or six other men in camp that he had counted earlier.

"And what might that be?" one said, a greedy look about him as he reached for the jug without waiting for the old mountain man to reply. Grabbing it from his hands, he pulled the cork out with his teeth, spit it off to the side, and took a long pull on the jug's contents. When he set the jug down, he stood up straight and had the most surprised look on his face that a body could imagine. Looking at him, you would swear he wanted to say something in the worst way but couldn't. He raised his eyebrows, his jaw dropped down to his belly button, and he looked as disbelieving as you might think possible.

"I tried telling you it wasn't nothing but sipping whiskey," Buckskin said. "But your amigo was a mite too quick to get it in him."

"Mostly, he don't know when to stop," Croft said, grabbing the jug out of his hand and sniffing its contents before taking a good long pull on it himself. His reaction was nearly the same as his friend's had been, although Croft seemed to be able to take it much easier than anyone else might.

Within five minutes everyone of Croft's friends had taken their share of the whiskey and the jug was nearly empty of its contents. Everyone except Kyle Garret himself had taken a taste of Buckskin's Taos Lightning. When he got the jug back in his possession, he corked it, sure that those who had drunk from it would sleep well that night. He was about to take the jug back to his possibles bag when he made a stop near Will and Hardy, who were still tied up.

"Your execution is sure enough on for tomorrow, boys," he said in a low voice, hoping these two were the only ones who would hear him speak. "I'll see can I have your horses ready to go when this crew starts breaking camp."

"Sounds good," Will said in agreement.

"Along with them horses, we could use a couple of six-guns," Bill Hardy said in a whisper no louder than Buckskin's. "We've still got unfinished business with these gents."

"I'll see what I can do," the old mountain man said as he left for his own horse as quickly as he had stopped. Doubtless, it would not be an easy job, but he'd try.

If Will and young Hardy slept at all that night, it was because they were tired and knew they would need the rest. Will continued to think of Margaret Ferris as he dozed off that night, wondering if he would ever see her again, sure in his mind what it was he would do if he did get out of this hellhole alive.

It was still dark when Buckskin nudged him and he came awake, suddenly aware that his hands were free as well as his feet. "This is the best I could do," the old-timer said as he silently laid each of their weapons down in between their legs.

"Reckon it'll do," Will whispered in appreciation.

"Don't you do nothing until the sun's up and they git ready to try something, understand?" Buckskin said, as though he were back in the old days and giving orders. "Not a move until then."

The dawn was breaking a short time later and once again it was Buckskin who brought Will and young Hardy plates of beans. Wanting to play along with whatever it was the old mountain man had in mind, they even let him spoon feed them while they acted as though they were bound just as tightly as they had been the night before. But even Will would have had to admit that one way or another he was getting anxious about getting out of this place. Patience was

160

getting to be something that only doctors had a lot of, as far as he was concerned.

Sure enough, Garret's men had hangovers from the small amount of drinking they had done the night before. All except for Garret himself, who seemed to be as alert as ever.

"Let's get this over with, Croft," Kyle Garret said as he cleaned off his plate and washed down his morning meal with the last of his coffee.

"You heard the boss," Croft then growled to one of his subordinates, who immediately got up and headed for Will Carston and Bill Hardy.

It was the last thing he ever did.

He reached down to pull Hardy up by an elbow, but before he could grasp the young gambler, Hardy had brought his six-gun up into his stomach and shot him once. The shot rang out throughout camp and the outlaw staggered back, clutching his stomach in pain as he fell to his knees. He was reaching for his six-gun when Hardy shot him a second time. This time the bullet went straight through his heart and killed him before he hit the ground.

Will rolled to his side, working himself to his knees as he took aim at the nearest member of the Garret crew and shot him twice too, killing him also. By the time his shots were off, there seemed to be lead flying everywhere about camp.

Buckskin materialized out of nowhere, the look on his face a determined one as he yelled out, "Croft!"

The big outlaw spun around, gun in hand and snapped a shot off at the old mountain man, hitting him in the pocket full of coins and knocking him backwards although not off his feet. But by then Buckskin had fired a shot of his own, hitting Croft in the throat, blood spurting from the outlaw's neck as he sank to the ground. However, the outlaw did manage to fire one more shot, which hit Buckskin and turned out to be fatal.

By the time the gunsmoke cleared there were four of Garret's gang who lay dead about the camp. Will thought he might have been nicked by a bullet and Hardy had some blood on him too, although it was hard telling where it had come from, whether it was his own or belonged to one of the others.

Buckskin was propped up against one of the rock walls, his chest and shirt filled with blood.

"I killed the son of a bitch, Marshal," he said weakly through lips that were red with blood he had coughed up. "Killed him, just like I said I would." This last sentence had a good deal of pride to it.

"You sure did, old-timer," Will said, knowing he could only make the man's death a little easier with his words.

"Trouble is, he killed me too." He looked at Will, as though his last words were meant to be meaningful ones. Grabbing hold of Will's shirtsleeve, he grumbled, "Ain't much in the way of survival, is it?" Then he fell over on his side, dead.

"Oh, I don't know, Buckskin, I'd say you done right well," was all Will could think to say to the dead man.

"Damn right," a determined looking Hardy said, as though for good measure.

Then it struck Will that he was forgetting something.

"Where's Garret? Did you get Garret?" he asked Hardy, knowing that must have been uppermost on the young gambler's mind.

"No. Did you?"

Together the two checked the dead bodies for Kyle Garret, but the gang leader was nowhere in sight.

"Damn it," Hardy whispered to himself. Then, looking at Will, he could see the same thing in the lawman's eyes that he himself was feeling.

Along with one of his other henchmen, Kyle Garret had gotten away!

"What do you say, pard?" Hardy said, quickly checking the loads of his six-gun.

"Let's saddle and ride!" was all he heard Will say as he did the same. He didn't seem to expect anything less.

CHAPTER

★ 20 ★

It only took Will a couple of minutes to find his horse and check his saddlebags for the extra cylinder he carried for his Remington .44. It was a habit he had picked up from Chance when his son had returned from the war. To hear him talk, Chance wouldn't have survived as many battles as he had if he hadn't had those extra cylinders he carried available to him. Still, he knew all too well that the time utilized in reloading his revolver was time he could not afford to waste.

"And where do you think you're going?" he asked Hardy when the young gambler grabbed the reins to his own mount.

Hardy gave Will a bewildered look, as though the man had gone daft.

"Why, saddle and ride," he said. "Ain't that what you just said back there? Saddle and ride?"

It was indeed what Will had said when the young man had asked him what they should do next. "Well, I changed my mind." Will Carston had never been one for fickleness or highmindedness. In fact, he was set in his ways about most things, not the least of which was saying what you do and doing what you say. But it was while he was reloading his Remington that the thought had hit him.

"Changed your mind! What are you, some kind of—"

"Look, sonny," Will said, mad now at being talked down to by this young whelp, "there's a helluva lot more than chasing after them horse thieves that needs doing here. And like it or not, you're the one who's gonna do it!"

"What the hell are you talking about?"

"I'm talking about rounding up the bodies of these would-be killers and draping 'em over a saddle and taking 'em back to that farmer we come on a while back. Lest you forgot, these are mostly his horses, and the ones that ain't was likely stole from someone else."

"What do I do with the bodies once I turn the horses over to the farmer?" Hardy asked. Will shook his head, wondering how the lad could be so good with his card game if he was this slow on the uptake of everything else.

"Hell, boy, double load 'em!" Will all but shouted, with a wave of the hand toward the dead bodies. "I wouldn't worry about any of them critters giving you any sass about it." Then, leaning down from his own horse, Will's voice lowered a good deal as he spoke to the young man in a confidential manner. "Of course, I'd make sure I'd taken their pistolas from 'em before I do. No telling when a body might decide to return to haunt you, now, is there?"

Bill Hardy was turning a dark shade of red as he said, "You've made your point." He was about to lead his horse away when he stopped and looked back at Will. "What about Buckskin?"

"I don't reckon he'll have much to say about being slung over a saddle either," was Will's reply. Glancing over at the lifeless body of the old mountain man, he shook his head. "If it weren't for the fact that he was misguided, I don't believe he was all that bad a man. Too bad the ground ain't softer, I'd give him a proper burial right here in the mountains."

"I'll make sure he gets a decent burial," Hardy said, as though he knew he'd never see Will Carston again.

"You do that, son, you do that. And son?"

"Yeah."

"When you git them horses to the farmer, take the bodies of these men in to Curious. Ary there's money on Kyle Garret's head, there might just as well be some on the likes of these yahoos too."

"I'll do that, Will," Hardy said. "You watch out for Kyle Garret. He's turned out to be slipperier than an eel."

Will smiled down at the lad. "Ain't that the truth?" This time it was he who turned to leave but stopped. "Tell you what, Billy," he added, using the young gambler's first name. "When you turn these bodies in to old Marshal Tub-of-Lard in Curious, you leave your name and an address I can reach you at if I don't catch up with you first. Like I say, there's money on Kyle Garret's head. When I catch up with him, I'll send it to you."

"You sound awful sure of yourself, Marshal," Hardy said with a bit of a cockeyed grin.

Will returned the smile. Thumbing the badge on his chest, he said to Hardy, "Believe me, son, this ain't a profession for doubters. Not at all."

"I think I understand," Hardy said to himself as he watched Will Carston ride out through the narrow ravine.

CHAPTER

★ 21 ★

Ransome Regret was beginning to dislike several of the citizens of Twin Rifles, particularly the pushy Deputy Marshal who had taken his pocket gun away. Who did he think he was, anyway? A hick deputy in a small town was all the man was, of that Regret was sure.

The boy he'd hired to go over to Kelly's Hardware to pick him up a six-gun had returned with the item and been satisfied with the dollar he had received for his troubles. In his room that night Regret had checked the cylinders and made sure the loads were all ready to be fired whenever they were needed, as he knew they would be. Still, the deputy lawman needed to be taught a lesson. You simply didn't push Ransome Regret around like that and get away with it. Why, no one had pushed him around like that since . . . well, for quite some time. The question was how would it be done?

It was with that thought in mind that he entered Ernie Johnson's Saloon the afternoon of the next day. The noon crowd had come and gone and it was too early for the evening crowd to begin ordering their drinks, so Regret thought the time ideal to get what he had come for, which was in reality anything but a drink.

"Afternoons must be pretty slow for you around here, barkeep," he said when Ernie had placed a beer before him at the bar. Normally, he would take a seat at a table and wait for someone to serve him there, but since the saloon was nearly empty he had decided to conduct his business bending an elbow at the bar, within easy earshot of the bartender.

"They can be," Ernie said in his usual cordial manner. He had found early on in his career as the proprietor of a saloon that it paid to at least be polite to the customers. After all, it was they who provided his livelihood, which was a thirst for some sort of liquid refreshment. It didn't pay to express your opinion of any of them—or on anything, for that matter—unless you were specifically asked.

Ernie went back to polishing shot glasses and was doing so in silence when Ransome Regret, half his beer gone, said, "You people seem like a pretty tightly knit group here."

Ernie frowned, a bit confused at the man's words. "I'm afraid I don't quite follow you, friend," he said, never once taking his eyes off the glasses he was polishing. As hard as he was polishing them, you'd think the man was intending to put them on display once he was through with them. Either that or he was bored stiff. Neither possibility was anything close to true. It was just that Ernie Johnson took a good deal of pride in his work.

"Oh, it seems to me that you stick up for one another quite a bit," Regret said. With a hint of a smile, he added, "Believe me, I got a first hand dose of it the other night in that card game."

Apparently, the man had taken the whole incident with a grain of salt, Ernie thought, which was good. A man had to have a sense of humor hereabouts to get through the day. "Yeah, I reckon we do, if you think about it." Ernie paused a moment before saying, "Of course, you won't find many who'll fault Joshua and Emmett on what they do."

"Is that right."

"Sure is. Pardee is just coming about to get himself a mite of respectability in Twin Rifles," Ernie said. He set the glass down and picked up another needing drying, beginning to work on it with his apron. "And Dallas, why, he ain't been here all that long. I reckon folks are still getting used to him. But he's a friend of Will Carston, so people are starting to accept him in this town." Ernie didn't have to see much from the corner of his eye to know that the City Marshal's name had brought a frown of sorts to Ransome Regret's face.

"Sounds like the lawmen in your fine community have made a lot of good friends," Regret said after trying his best to gain his composure. If he had remembered Margaret Ferris with a thought of lust, his memory of Will Carston held as much hate as it had for Abel Ferris. Perhaps he too would be in need of being taught a lesson. But first things first. It was the

170

deputy who needed to be taught a lesson at the moment.

"Mostly, I reckon that's right."

Regret took another sip of beer and raised a curious eyebrow. "Mostly?"

"Oh, yeah. There's some who live on the outskirts of town and don't have much use for the law and Twin Rifles," Ernie said. Then, with a shake of his head, he added, "Take those Hadley Brothers. They can be a mean bunch when they want to. Mighty mean."

Regret's eyes lit up with almost as much excitement as they had when he had first seen Margaret Ferris after all these years. The thought ran through his mind that he had found what he had come for.

"And these dreadful fellows live outside the limits of your fair city, you say?" Regret was doing his best to contain the enjoyment he was feeling within himself.

"Yeah, about three miles east of here." Ernie set down the shot glass and began working on another one.

Regret finished his beer and coughed as he set down his beer mug. When Ernie offered a refill, he silently shook his head. "No thanks," he finally said. "But I'll tell you what I would like. I think I've got a bit of a cold coming on. If you've got it, I'd like a bottle of your best," he said, sliding ten dollars in coin across the bar at Ernie. "Perhaps I'll make myself a hot toddy tonight before I retire."

Ernie was impressed with any man who would willingly offer to pay ten dollars for a bottle of his whiskey and made no bones about handing a bonded bottle to Regret, who seemed to be in an awful hurry to leave. But then, Ernie thought to himself, he would be too if he were in a hurry to vacate the place and didn't want to spread a cold around. The trouble was, Ransome Regret didn't act a whole hell of a lot like he had a cold. Not until he had finished his beer, anyway.

Out of curiosity, Ernie Johnson placed himself right inside the batwing doors to his saloon for the next fifteen minutes. After all, there wasn't anyone else in the place to serve, so his time was his own, wasn't it? And just as he had suspected, it was at the end of that fifteen minutes that Regret, cold or not, came loping by on a horse, likely rented from the livery, and headed out of town. When he was past Ernie Johnson's Saloon, Ernie stepped out onto the boardwalk and followed man and horse out of town.

Just as he had suspected, once past the city limits, Ransome Regret had reined his horse to the east.

"Cold, my ass," Ernie muttered to himself in disgust as he went back to his saloon.

Regret found Ernie Johnson's information to be as reliable as any town gossip. He chuckled to himself as he neared the rather run-down structure that served as a house to the Hadley Brothers. All five of them. All a man needed to know to get by in a town, no matter what its size, was how to find the local bartender or the local gossip. Hell, they were both the same thing, weren't they? The old biddy would be the one who got the dirt on the women in town, while the bartender was the one who heard the men's side of it all.

A big oversized man was out in front of the house and appeared to be chopping firewood as Regret pulled his reins in at the abode.

He smiled his best smile as he said, "Would this be the Hadley residence?"

Carny Hadley, the oldest of the Hadley Brothers, set down the axe he was working with. "If you're looking for the Hadley's, you've found 'em. And this is where we live," he said, tossing a thumb over his shoulder at the house. "As for a residence, I couldn't tell you for sure. All I know is it keeps most of the rain out when it storms."

"I see." Regret found himself wondering just how hard it would be to do business with these people. The smile was still on his face, but it seemed to be a little bit harder to keep there.

"If you're selling, I ain't got the money to buy," Carny said, any humor he might have had now gone.

The form of another big man filled the doorway to the house. This one was nearly as big as the first one and sported a lever action rifle which lay in the crook of his arm. "And if you're collecting," Wilson Hadley, the second oldest of the five brothers, said, a mean look about him, "well, you'd better find a new profession." At this last, Wilson pulled back the hammer of the rifle, producing a cocking noise that was quite disturbing to Regret.

"Easy now, friend," Regret said, slowly getting off his horse. "I haven't come to do you any harm. And I might be able to help you out in the way of money."

"Now that'll be a first," Carny said with a snarl. "Ain't never seen a body yet come up to me and flat out offer me money. Have you, Wilson?"

"Not hardly," his brother said with a similar tone to his voice. "Ain't natural for a man in these parts."

Regret gave a simple shrug and reached for his saddlebag.

Wilson Hadley moved the aim of his rifle directly toward Regret. "If what comes out of that saddlebag looks anything like a pistol or any other weapon I know of, you'll die in your tracks, mister."

"Believe me, it's not," Regret assured the man and

slowly pulled out the bottle of whiskey he had purchased at Ernie Johnson's saloon. "I simply thought we might be able to discuss some business over a drink or two."

"Just what kind of business you got in mind, mister?" Carny was suddenly drawn to the man, or at least the prospect of putting a few dollars in his pocket.

"Cups are inside," Wilson grumbled before Regret could answer and disappeared from the doorway, as though this were Regret's invitation to enter the Hadley quarters.

All they had to drink from were crude tin coffee cups, but Regret was sure that to these men it was the finest service. He filled their cups, only half filling his own, making a mental note not to drink any more of the whiskey than he had to in order to get this deal made.

"Ernie Johnson's brew, eh?" Wilson said after drinking half his cup of whiskey in one swallow.

"Yup, that's Ernie's stuff all right," Carny agreed, drinking just as much as his brother. Neither one seemed to be affected by the strength of the whiskey, which was considerable.

"I understand that you gentlemen don't always get along with the law in Twin Rifles," Regret said after refilling both the brothers' cups.

"Could be." Carny gave a suspicious squint at the stranger sitting at their table. "What's it to you?"

"Nothing. But it might be worth a hundred dollars to you," Regret said, at which point he lifted a small leather sack from his coat pocket, undid the ties and poured five twenty-dollar gold pieces on the table before Carny and Wilson. The way the two men eyed the coins, you'd have thought they'd never seen that kind of money in their entire lives. And they hadn't. At least, not a hundred dollars all at one time.

Once Wilson managed to focus his eyeballs, he drank the entire contents of his coffee cup, belched, and said, "Now you're talking my language, mister."

"I do believe my brother's got a point," Carny said, taking the lead. "Now then, what is it you need done?"

Regret scooped up three of the gold pieces and placed them back in the leather sack, placing it back in his coat pocket.

"If you agree to what I have in mind, I'll leave these here as an advance," Regret said, all business now. "You'll get the rest when the job is done. Now then, I have a plan. Here's what I want you two to do . . ."

When he got through explaining, Regret and Carny and Wilson Hadley had a deal. Which says a lot for what money will do to a man.

CHAPTER
★ 22 ★

Riding out of that ravine wasn't any easier than entering it had been, but Will Carston took his time just the same. No use in seeing how easy a body could get his horse to go lame on him now, was there? Or, just as bad, picking up something in the horse's shoe that had to be taken care of and could, eventually if not taken care of pronto, cause the horse to go as lame as anything else might. No, sir, he told himself, there would be plenty of time to catch up with this yahoo once he made it to the open plains. Of course, there was also the very real fact that Kyle Garret would be riding just as hard to get away from him. But Will tried to put that thought out of his mind.

When he reached the opening to the ravine, and then the area of the cave they had stayed in a couple of nights back, Will was surprised to see that Kyle Garret had begun to follow his own back trail; or at least what was left of it. The storm that he and Buckskin and young Hardy had experienced had washed out all evidence of any tracks. But that didn't matter to Will, for he had learned long ago that it was important that a man watch his back trail. Things always looked different when you rode in the opposite direction. So along with the fact that he was a bit of an expert in this area of tracking, coupled with the fact that Kyle Garret was leaving a trail that was all but impossible to cover up in all this half-dried mud, he would have no trouble at all tracking down the outlaw.

"No trouble at all, you sorry bastard," he mumbled to himself as he looked out across the open plains area and the trail that even a blind man could follow. At first the words surprised him, and he couldn't believe he'd said them. Not that Will wasn't known to cuss once in a while. It was just that one usually had to push pretty far to get him to use that kind of vocabulary.

As he rode out after Garret, he found himself reasoning that it must have been because Kyle Garret had been responsible for the death of Buckskin. Hell, the man was mostly harmless other than the fact that he was pretty much full of himself when it came to the area of tracking and his expertise in it. Or being a used-to-was mountain man, for that matter. Will had started his life doing just that, but had the good sense to get out of the Rockies once the beaver were gone. There were, he'd found out, plenty of other places on this frontier that needed looking after, not to mention plenty of other jobs. And there was Cora back in St. Louis and more and more he had pined for her as the long winters and the longer years went by. As for old

Buckskin, like he'd said to Hardy back there, the man wasn't all that bad. Besides, he had always found it hard to talk down to a man who had saved his life. And there had been more than a few of those.

The sun was out and shining by then and he enjoyed the warmth of it as he continued to track Garret and his compadre, although he still wasn't sure who that could be. But then, he didn't recall seeing any of the outlaw's faces long enough to really take notice of them while he'd been tied up in Garret's camp. His mind had been too consumed with how he would get out of that fix to notice much else.

It was approaching noon when he pulled his horse to a stop, about a hundred yards off a small rise in the distance. He had no intention of stopping for a dry camp, although he likely should have. It was Kyle Garret that was on his mind now and he was sure that he could catch up with him soon if he kept at it, kept tracking the man.

He was pulling off his buckskin jacket, having in mind to stow it until later in the day when nightfall came, when a shot rang out from the rise. In an instant, Will's horse gave a buck, tried to rear itself, and fell to the ground. Twitching and neighing, the horse was obviously in pain, but it wasn't until Will was able to work himself free of the saddle he had gone down on that he noticed the blood spurting from his mount's right leg like a river out of control after a flash flood.

Will threw his jacket down on the saddle and reached for his Henry rifle, now in its scabbard, as a second shot rang out. He felt himself jerk to the side some as he raised his rifle and sought out the man shooting at him.

"Son of a bitch," he mumbled, standing there in the

open like a damn fool, making himself available to the shooter for one more shot. But the shot never came and all he could do was stand there in frustration and feel like a fool, for he could do nothing else.

Leaning the rifle down against the horse's belly, the butt of it stuck in the mud and sand but easily available to him, he knelt down and examined the horse's wound. "Got you good, old fella," he said quietly with a sad shake of his head. He'd had this horse for several years and it had been a good one, the two of them getting along almost as well as he did with some humans. Hell, better in some cases, that was for sure. "Yes, sir, got you good, they did."

The bullet had broken the leg and the horse was bleeding to death to boot. And busted bones on a horse, well, they just didn't mend. Not so they would be any good again. Will looked down into the sad eyes of the horse, almost sure those were tears coming from its eyes now. He knew good and well that the wounded animal must be feeling as sad as he was himself. He ran a sleeve under his nose, thankful that at least no one else was here to see the way he was acting. Will was a strong man and the only time he could remember crying was when his Cora had died, and that had been in private. A man simply didn't show emotions like that in public, or at all. It just wasn't done. Still, he felt an awful lot like he had a runny nose, as though he had a cold or something. But when he pulled a handkerchief out of his back pocket with one hand and his Remington out of his holster with the other, he knew good and damn well having a cold had nothing to do with what was taking place here and now.

"You know, old fella, I've had a lot of horses shot out from under me, yes I have," he said, still speaking in a low tone of voice, as though the whole conversation were private, just between him and the horse. But as tough as Will Carston was, he felt a tear well up in his eye as he said, "But I never had to kill a horse I had. And I sure hate doing this."

Then he cocked the revolver, pointed it at the horse's head, and killed it with one shot.

Will was still standing there an hour later when young Bill Hardy rode up, leading the string of horses from Kyle Garret's camp. He gave a sigh of relief when he saw the lawman standing there next to his dead horse, his Henry rifle in the crook of his arm, as though he were ready to go on the hunt.

"I heard shots," Hardy said.

"Well, at least your ears ain't failed you," Will said in a testy tone of voice.

"I take it they ambushed you."

"You could say that. Got away too," Will said, no change in his tone. "One thing's for sure, though."

"Obviously, we're close to 'em."

Will looked at the lad as though he were daft. "Hell, I know that, you fool!"

"Then what are you talking about, Marshal?" Hardy asked, a bit confused as to the man's reasoning.

"Why, I'm gonna kill him, that's what!" Will said, raising the rifle in the air like a Comanche warrior on the prod.

"You're gonna kill Kyle Garret because he shot you?"

"Shot me?" Will looked his body over, not finding any blood until he got to his left arm, at which time he noticed the sleeve down to his elbow soaked a deep red color that could only be blood. "When the hell did that happen?" he asked himself in true puzzlement.

"Likely when those birds were shooting at you,

Marshal," Hardy said as he dismounted and pulled out a big red bandana as he approached Will. "I never did take to carrying the kind of homemade brew old Buckskin did, and I never did chew, so this will have to do. If you can stand it, that is." This last was meant as a personal dig at the lawman, if a bit on the humorous side. The question was whether Will Carston was capable of showing a sense of humor at this time.

He wasn't.

"Just tie the damn thing above the wound someplace and point me to one of these nags you're pulling along so I can saddle it," Will growled cantankerously.

Hardy chuckled as he tied the bandana around Will's arm. "You're some piece of work, Will." he said with a hint of a smile.

"And what's that supposed to mean?"

"Why, here you are a lawman, where gitting shot at is all part of the job, and you're acting like it's some sort of grudge you've got against this fella for shooting you."

"Look son," Will said, his mood changing from cantankerous to downright angry. "It ain't that I mind getting shot at, although I do, you understand. But this here horse of mine didn't just up and keel over for lack of energy, you know. That son of a bitch Garret, he shot him out from under me. That's why I'm going after him and that's why he's gonna die the next time I see him. Understand?"

Hardy smiled and shook his head back and forth in disbelief. "Like I said, Will, you're some piece of work."

"Oh, shut up and git me one of them nags," Will muttered.

CHAPTER
★ 23 ★

Margaret Ferris was in her kitchen, helping Rachel with a meatloaf she had been working on nearly all day. Her daughter had become quite proficient at adapting some of Margaret's own recipes over the years, and the meatloaf was one of them. The mother had yet to find out specifically what it was that her daughter put in the preparation that gave it a slightly different taste than her own concoction. On the other hand, she wasn't about to complain about it, for none of the customers who sat at their community table ever found fault with the dish.

"I swear if you ever get Chance to put a ring on your finger, Rachel, you'll make him a fine wife," Margaret said with a smile that held a good deal of pride, as she took a whiff of the aroma that now filled the air.

Rachel turned from her work, a blushing red now filling her face. "Oh, Mama, you're just saying that." Her smile was a bit sheepish but not unusual to Margaret for she had always known her daughter would be the shy one of the family. All except when it came to being around Chance Carston of late. When she was around that man, why, her whole personality seemed to change in a way Margaret had never seen before. It was as though she were . . . well, aggressive for want of a better term. And for the life of her, Margaret couldn't understand it. Oh, she could remember those early years with Abel so long ago, but she had never categorized herself as being anything close to aggressive. Now that he was gone, well, that was a whole different matter. A woman making her way through the business world all alone, yes, that was an entirely different matter.

"No, dear, I'm not just saying that," Margaret said as she placed an arm around her daughter and gave her a loving squeeze. "I meant every word of it, and you know it."

"Yes, Mama." Still blushing, Rachel's tone had become even lower than before. She turned back to her work on the meal she was preparing. "I'd better get back to this food. Two more hours and supper will be on us."

Margaret nodded agreement. "And so will the customers." She looked out the back window and added, "I see Mr. Bodeen is still hard at work."

"Yes, ma'am. He does almost as good a job at chopping the deadwood as Mr. Will."

Still looking at the old mountain man, Margaret fought to maintain her image of a tough-minded woman. Until recently she had been successful with Will's old friend, Dallas Bodeen. It was when she had broken down the other day and, to her surprise, he had taken her in his arms, it was since then that she had found it increasingly awkward to try to put on a hard face to this man. Just thinking about it conjured up mixed emotions in her about how she was feeling about various people. Feeling a sniffle come to her nose, she dabbed it with her hanky. "Don't forget, that man eats his share of food too."

"He sure does, Mama."

"In fact, in all my born days I can't recall anyone who eats more than the men on this frontier, from your father and Will to everyone in between."

Rachel gave her mother a warm smile. "Yes, Mama." The thought of her father had conjured up warm memories she sometimes thought she had forgotten. But they were still there. They would be there until she died.

"I'll set the table and be back to help you with those biscuits and some of those pies, dear," Margaret said briskly, grabbed a towel filled with freshly dried eating utensils and headed for the community table.

No one was seated at the table and she had no trouble setting places for the number of visitors she was expecting for supper that night. She found that she often enjoyed these times when she was alone and doing little chores such as this. It often gave her pause to think of how lucky she really was, even with Abel gone. But lately she also discovered that her thoughts had been turning to Will Carston, who she had grown quite fond of since her husband's death and even more fond of when Will's own wife was killed by the Comancheros. She wondered now if perhaps that was the reason she seemed to understand Rachel and her feelings for Chance Carston. Not because she, Margaret, had been through the same thing with her own beau so long ago, as her daughter obviously assumed, but because she was beginning to feel the very same way about Chance's father, Will. As she continued to set the table, she decided it was something to think about—and perhaps even discuss with Will—at a later date.

She jumped when she felt the hands on her waist and it scared her. It wasn't because they were big hands so much as the fact that they had grabbed her from behind.

"Oh, it's you," she said when she turned to see Ransome Regret standing there with an ear-to-ear grin. "Please don't do that."

But Regret seemed not to hear her words. At least if he did, he didn't grasp the meaning they contained. "Just like old times, isn't it Margaret?" he said, the grin now a leer.

"No," she said with a shaky voice, a touch of fear noticeable in her tone. "All you did when you came to town was bring back the past. And all I want to do, Rance, is forget it. Do you understand? I just want to forget it!" She hadn't thought about the near rape in years, but ever since Ransome Regret had shown up the past had been ever present in her mind.

The leer seemed to take on an evilness all its own now, if that was possible. Margaret had seen it only once before and of late she couldn't get it out of her mind. "You know, Margaret, of all those women, I've always loved kissing you the most," Regret said. Margaret didn't like it, didn't like his look at all, and thought it was time to let him know it.

She slapped him hard enough to visibly rotate his head a half right turn. The echo was as loud as a gunshot, filling the room with its sound. But it wiped the grin or leer or whatever you wanted to call it off Ransome Regret's face.

"So that's how it's going to be," he growled, his tone changed considerably. He also seemed more determined than ever to have his way with her, just as she had remembered him from so long ago.

"No!" she tried to scream but before she could get it all out, her voice was muffled by his kiss. It was a hard, forced kiss, nothing at all romantic about it, just as vicious and insensitive as before.

He had hold of her by the shoulders and had pushed her all the way over, her back on the community table, when Rachel stepped through the kitchen door. "Mother!" she yelled with a shriek, then quickly disappeared back into the kitchen area. If Ransome Regret heard her at all, he didn't notice, for he kept right on forcing himself on Margaret.

"You no good son of a bitch!" was all Regret heard when he felt the big hand of Dallas Bodeen grasp his shoulder and pull him off the woman he was enjoying kissing so much.

Dallas wasted few words once he had Regret off Margaret, who seemed more shaken up than anything else. If anything, it was Margaret who had hurt Regret for the man had several nail marks on his face, wounds put there by Miss Margaret he was sure.

Dallas hit Regret hard across the face, knocking him back across the hallway and into a wall. By the time the man bounced off the wall, Dallas had hit him again in the same place, drawing a bit of blood this time. Regret made the mistake of feeling his bloodied lip, which gave the old mountain man enough time to batter the man's innards some with two or three hard swings. He was wobbly on his legs and weak as a kitten when Dallas had him by the back of the neck and was guiding him toward the entrance of the Ferris House.

Joshua was just entering the Ferris House when he heard Dallas growling, "I'll kill you," when he saw the mountain man hit Regret in the mouth, sending the man sprawling through the doorway and onto the boardwalk.

Brushing past Joshua as though he didn't even exist, Dallas followed Regret outside. Pointing a hard, stubby finger at the man on the boardwalk, he snarled in a low even tone, "If they's nothing you never forget, Regret, you make sure it's that. You come anywhere close to Miss Margaret again and I swear I'll kill you. Deader'n gone beaver is what you'll be."

No sooner did he turn around to go back in to the Ferris House than Dallas ran smack dab into Margaret. But getting run into isn't where it stopped. She grabbed him by his buckskin jacket, stood on tiptoes, and kissed Dallas on the mouth so hard the old mountain man felt woozy when their lips parted.

"Lordy," was all he could say as he looked down at her in surprise.

"Why did you do that?" an irritated and sore Regret said, slowly getting to his feet and just as shocked as Dallas.

"Why, it's simple, you stupid knothead," Joshua drawled in his back hills tone. "Old Dallas just proved they's still a code of honor out here when it comes to the way you treat ladies." To Dallas, he added, "That is what it was all about, weren't it? Onliest thing I got to see was the last of it, you know."

"Honor be damned!" Dallas grumbled at Regret with a frown. "She just kissed me to prove that she'd rather kiss an ugly old bag of dirt like me than a pretty-faced, black-hearted son of a bitch like you."

Joshua chuckled at Regret, taking in the sight of him. "Trouble is you ain't no pretty face no more, are ye?"

"Come inside, Dallas," Margaret said, trying to act as though nothing had happened. "I'll fix up your hand. It looks like it's bleeding in spots."

Actually, it was Ransome Regret's blood that was on his hand and Dallas had an idea that both of them knew it as she led him back inside the Ferris House.

It wasn't until later, at the supper meal, that Joshua mentioned that the last he'd seen of Regret that afternoon was when he'd mounted his horse and ridden out of town, heading to the east. What he didn't tell them was that he suspected the man was headed for the Hadley Brothers and their homestead.

Ernie Johnson had told him so.

CHAPTER

★ 24 ★

They tracked Kyle Garret and his cohort until sundown of that day. And even if the man had another hour's jump on them, they were sure that they had made up time once Will had gotten atop one of the "nags" he complained about after his own horse had been shot out from under him.

Actually, the mounts he had to choose from were anything but nags. Whoever the men were who had owned them—presumably the laggards now draped over the saddles of more than a couple of the horses— at least they had a good knowledge of horseflesh when they picked these mounts. Odds were they had likely stolen the horses to begin with, but at least they knew when to pick a good riding horse to steal. You had to give them that, Will thought to himself.

"Ary we don't catch him outright tomorrow morning, I figure we'll come on that farmer and we can get rid of at least his horses," Will said as they stopped to make camp that night.

"That ought to lighten our load considerably," Hardy said in agreement as he went about checking the horses and taking care of them as best he could. Getting water to them after a day like today was the most important thing to do. They could nibble on whatever grass he could find to stake them out near right now. And if that farmer had any sense, he'd give these mounts of his a good rubdown and a fair ration of oats once they were back in his possession.

Will set to boiling some coffee over the fire he'd built and threw some thick slabs of bacon on his fry pan. Along with a couple of hardtack biscuits it would make a passable evening meal. Besides, he'd had his fill of beans for a mite. One of Margaret's steaks or roasts would taste mighty good about now, but bacon and hardtack would do for a substitute.

"I wonder where old Garret is headed now?" Hardy asked when he'd returned from taking care of the horses. Squatting down, he took the plate Will offered with a cup of coffee, eating the meal slowly even though he was quite hungry. They had not, after all, taken time to make noon camp. And as hungry as he was, perhaps eating the food slowly would make his stomach believe it was a greater amount than it was.

Will pushed his hat back on his head and took a sip of coffee, obviously thinking hard before he gave an answer. "I don't know how good you are at watching your back trail, son, but that's what we've been following ever since we left Garret's hideout this morning," he said.

"I thought some of this looked familiar," Hardy

said, a bit of awe in his voice. Then, taking in some of the surroundings and recognizing them for what they were, he added, "Yeah, now I know where we are. But what's that got to do with anything?"

"Well, that puzzled me at first," Will replied, taking a chew of the rather crisp bacon. "I figured maybe he'd rid out of that ravine like a bat out of hell and lit a shuck for hell knows where. But after a while, I knew he was following his back trail, even though there wasn't no tracks to follow. Seems to me now he's a-headed back toward that town I chased him out of, that place called Curious."

"Hmm." Hardy seemed to find this only slightly amusing. Or was it just that he was more interested in his food at the moment? Likely the food, Will thought. "Think he might know someone back in Curious, do you?" the young gambler asked around a mouthful of food.

Will shrugged noncommittally. "Could be, but if he does it sure beats the living hell outta me, son."

When they were through eating, they tossed around the possibilities each had thought of concerning who it might be that Kyle Garret was going back to in Curious, a town that didn't seem too curious at all once you thought of it. It wasn't long before the subject matter sort of dried up, and so did the conversation.

The next morning they were up early, eating a skimpy breakfast of hardtack and coffee before saddling up and heading out after Kyle Garret again. The sun was hotter today and there wasn't a sign of a cloud in the sky, nor was there a wind. Will found himself thinking that back in Twin Rifles this might be a nice day for an afternoon picnic with a lady friend.

"What're you smiling at?" Hardy asked as he mounted up.

"Just foolishness, lad, just foolishness," Will smiled. Once in the saddle, he realized that any thoughts of a picnic would have to wait. Right now he had to finish tracking down Kyle Garret and his friend.

They rode their horses hard that morning, Will staying out front of Hardy as the gambler struggled to keep up with the lawman and keep his horses in tow. Every once in a while Will would stop near a pile of horse apples while he waited for Hardy to catch up with him. It not only gave his horse a breather, but held an important lesson for young Hardy, if he cared to listen.

"We're gaining on 'em," Will said about mid-morning at one of his stops.

"How can you tell?" Hardy asked, letting his own horse stop for a few minutes.

"Horse apples," the lawman said and held out a fistful of horse droppings. "Gitting softer faster the farther we go. Ain't had much time to dry, you know."

"Let me see that."

It was a fatal mistake, for Will plopped the horse apples right in the gambler's hand. And when he did, he smiled.

"What's so funny?"

"I wonder what them friends of yours with the pasteboards would say ary they seen you holding a piece of horseshit instead of a deck of cards?" Will chuckled.

Hardy looked down at the stuff in his hand as though it were some vile matter, which in a way it was, and tossed it aside. He might be young, but he wasn't all that inexperienced.

"Fact of the matter is, Marshal, that's usually what some of my friends with the pasteboards accuse me of dealing 'em sometimes," he said with a slight smile.

"At least you've got a sense of humor, son," Will said and shook his head and put his horse at a gallop, trailing Kyle Garret once again.

It was close to noon when Will came on the farmer and the red barn he remembered so well. This time the old man met them in his front yard with a Spencer rifle in the crook of his arm, a scowl on his face.

"You again!"

"That's right, friend. And I'm still chasing that same yahoo I was before. Do have some good news for you though," Will said, dismounting and loosening the cinch on his horse so he could blow.

"And vat could dat possibly be?" The man was a pure cynic, of that Will was certain.

"In a few minutes my partner oughtta be coming over that same rise I did, and he'll be bringing back most of your horses, I do believe."

Rather than say a simple thank you, the man grumbled, "Vell, it's about time."

"And you're quite welcome, sir." After a moment of silence, he added, "I don't suppose you've seen those fellas I've been following ride through, have you?" He knew good and well the two outlaws had been by here, for their tracks had led here as plain as day. He just wanted to see what kind of a rise he could get out of this farmer, see what he had to say about them.

"Ya, day vas here, same damn fools as before. Und like before, they vant my horses, but vat can I do? 'You already tooken 'em! Vat more do you vant?' I say." The farmer threw his hands up in the air in a gesture of pure frustration. "Und off they go, riding like scared jackrabbits. Damn fools."

"Well, we got your horses back, friend," Will said again by way of reassurance.

It wasn't long before Bill Hardy and his horses came riding into the farmer's yard. Without a word of greeting, the German strode through the lot of horses, searching for his own. When he found his mount, he led it off to his corral. When he returned, he didn't look pleased at all.

"Mr. Lawman, you still owe me a horse," he said in a stern manner. "I only got vun and day tooken two."

"Must be the one Garret's riding," Will said.

"Den you get him and bring me back my horse, by Got!" This time he slammed a fist into the palm of his hand to emphasize his point.

"Now mister, you just simmer down there," Will said, looking down on the shorter man, a stern look on his own face as he spoke. This was authority speaking now, and Will wanted the man to know it. "What you need to do is learn how to be grateful for what you've got."

"And vat do I got besides not all my horses?" the man said, uppity as can be.

"I'll tell you what you got, mister," Hardy said, a frown coming to his own face now. "You got half of your horses what were stole back in good shape. And you got me and the marshal here hunting up the last of your precious stock. Now, I was you, I'd bite down real hard on my words and chew on 'em a helluva lot more afore I went spitting 'em out like bullets. 'Cause just like them ricochets, why, they might come flying right back at you. Yes, sir." A wink and a nod put the topping on what he had in mind to say. You'd think the young lad had been watching Will and old Buckskin. And, in fact, he had.

"Come on, Hardy," Will said as he pulled his reins

to go. "This ungrateful old coot likely don't do nothing but complain just to hear hisself talk, living alone and all."

"I'll say," was Hardy's reply as he pulled his remaining horses along behind him. "A woman would have to be awful hard put to marry into a stubborn old fool like that."

CHAPTER

★ 25 ★

They had only been on the trail for half an hour when Hardy pulled his horse to a halt. Will hadn't been riding all that hard, so when he looked over his shoulder and saw the young gambler sitting atop his mount as though he had all the time in the world, he waved him to come ahead and gave his own horse a bit of rest while young Hardy moved up beside him.

"What's the matter, boy, you feeling sickly or something, are you?" Will asked, obviously irritated. "Horse throw a shoe? What?"

"It's like this, Marshal. My stomach's telling me what little we had for a morning meal ain't too awful much about now, figuring it's after noon at least." Almost as if it were done on command, Bill Hardy's stomach growled as though it hadn't been fed in a week and a half.

"Young pups," Will grumbled to himself. "Look, sonny, I spent a goodly number of years in the Texas Rangers, and when we were hot on a man's trail, why, we kept on a-going until we got our man or we couldn't see no more to ride. Now, I know what you're stomach's saying cause mine's singing the same song. But damn it, boy, if we give these yahoos any more time, why, they'll ride clean to Mexico before you know it!"

"But Will—"

"But, my ass!" the lawman interrupted in anger. "I swear the young 'uns of your generation can't even keep up with an old fart like me. Tell you what, Hardy, you sit you down and take you a dry camp for however long you need to get into the sort of things. Me, I'm tracking this son of a bitch down before the sun sets, and ary I don't plant him by the time Old Sol dies today, I'll at least stop his heart from beating."

With that the lawman wheeled his horse about and headed off after Kyle Garret at a full gallop, leaving nothing more than a cloud of dust.

Bill Hardy dismounted and took his canteen from his saddle. Taking off his hat, he turned it upside down and poured some water in it to let his horse drink. Then he took a swallow himself.

Staring after the cloud of dust, his face turning red with anger, he said, "Can't keep up with an old fart like him, huh? Well, I'll show the old bastard. Yeah, I'll show him a thing or two!"

It was close to the evening meal when Will Carston pulled into the town of Curious. There seemed to be a fair amount of people on the boardwalks, apparently getting ready to close up their shops or quitting a mite early today. But for a town called Curious, they didn't seem to care much about who had just ridden into their fair borough. It puzzled Will, it purely did.

He still had Kyle Garret on his mind, but there was something else he needed to tend to first. As hard and fast as he had ridden, he had done a lot of jostling around in the saddle, and it had aggravated his wound something fierce. So much that he thought it had started to bleed again, although he realized it had never been sewn up. Still, even a flesh wound could get infected and if that happened a body could be in real trouble. Men had gotten everything from toes to legs and arms amputated because an infection that hadn't been treated proper had set in. And as much as he wanted the skin of that outlaw, there was no use taking a chance on trading his capture for an infected wound. So he headed for Doc Miles and his office, hoping the physician was still in.

He was.

"Howdy, Doc," he said as he entered the doctor's outer office.

"Good afternoon," the man said. Will couldn't tell whether the man was simply tired or whether he had suddenly gotten nervous about something. "What can I do for you, Marshal?"

"It's this shoulder of mine, Doc. Got me a flesh wound while I was shooting it out with that outlaw I'm tracking," Will said. "All I had time to do was wrap a bandana around it and pray hard I wouldn't bleed to death."

"And apparently you haven't bled to death," the doctor said, taking in the sight of the wound and the bandana covering it.

"That's a fact. But it sure did start aching me some this afternoon. Figured I'd stop by and get it taken care of before it got infected bad."

"Don't you worry about him." Will heard the words before he saw the speaker, but it didn't take two shakes before the man had entered from the room the doctor kept for doing serious medical work.

It was Kyle Garret! He had a six-gun in his hand and it was trained right at Will's stomach.

"You get back in there and get that bullet outta Jake," the outlaw growled. "This one can bleed to death for all I care."

Will could tell Doc Miles wanted to say something to the outlaw in the worst way, for no man likes being pushed around on his own territory, and this was the doctor's territory. Instead, the older man bit his lip and silently went back to his operating room.

Will could have kicked himself for not figuring out why it was Garret would be coming back to Curious. It was so simple! Apparently, either Hardy or Buckskin or Will had hit Jake, Kyle Garret's cohort in crime, but Will hadn't noticed it during the shootout back at the outlaw's hideout. It wasn't that Garret had known anyone in this sleepy little town. It was just the fact that this was the nearest town with a doctor in it. Well, at least the man was loyal to his own men, which was more than you could say for a lot of outlaws.

"Come on, lawman," Garret growled at Will, yanking Will's six-gun from his holster. "Where you're going, you ain't gonna have to worry about whether or not that wound gets fixed or not." With his six-gun, Garret motioned Will out the door of the doctor's office. "You make a move that looks anything even close to being what it ain't supposed to be and I'll kill you where you stand."

"Right," Will said, indicating he understood the man's instructions.

Once down on the boardwalk, he was instructed to take a left and began slowly walking although he wasn't sure where his destination was. And at the moment he didn't really care. All he had on his mind was getting out from under the gun of this man who was known to kill people in their tracks. The memory of what young Hardy had told Will about how Kyle Garret had killed his friend in cold blood now stood out in Will's mind. Perhaps too much.

What also stood out in his mind—perhaps more so than anything else—was the most painful question he thought he had ever encountered: Was this the last time he'd ever be able to remember the thought of Margaret Ferris and what he was sure was a growing love he had for her? Had he seen her for the last time? He found himself desperately hoping it wasn't so.

With that in mind, he tried to figure out how he would get out of this fix. How could he stay alive? How could he get back to Margaret? How—

"FILL YOUR HAND, YOU SON OF A BITCH!" The voice belonged to Bill Hardy and it came from his left in the meanest growl he had ever heard from the young gambler.

They had walked only the distance in front of the building on which Doc Miles's second-floor office stood, and come upon an alley between this and the next building. It was here that Will heard the hate-filled voice of Hardy, and here that he turned to see him.

The young gambler stood there in the alleyway all alone, his six-gun draped at his side in its holster. You'd swear he had taken a stance not dissimilar to the kind of trash they printed in those dime novels, the way he was standing there. And he didn't make a move until Kyle Garret, who already had a gun out and pointed at Will's back, made the fool mistake of swinging his own pistol over toward Hardy. What happened next, Will couldn't believe.

Young Bill Hardy pulled his six-gun out with what those dime novels liked to call "greased lightning." He had it out and fired from the hip just as Garret's gun went off, shooting high and wild and knocking Hardy's hat from his head. But Hardy's aim was true and the bullet hit Garret in the chest. Just one was all it took. Will was sure the man was dead by the time he fell to the boardwalk.

Hardy was holstering his six-gun when the window pane of Doc Miles's one window to his operating room shattered. The window faced the alleyway and splinters of glass flew out and down into the alley as a bleeding man who could only have been Jake appeared in the window, gun in hand.

"Look out!" Will yelled, but it was too late. Jake, Garret's wounded cohort, had poked his pistol through the window and shot Hardy high in the upper chest. Just below the shoulder, Will thought.

But before the young gambler could pull his gun a second time and avenge his would-be assassin, a shotgun blast erupted inside the operating room. The blast took Jake in the back and propelled him halfway out the window, where he slumped over dead.

As the echoes of gunshots died away in the alleyway and several of the townspeople began to show themselves, Will thought he heard old Doc Miles inside his operating room. And he could swear he heard Doc grumble, "Break my pane window, will you!"

"Old Doc, he means business all right." The voice came from behind him and Will turned to see the wide pot-bellied shape of the town marshal, Todd Harlon.

"I reckon he does," Will said in agreement. Then, to Harlon, he added, "Say, is this the only time you show up around here? When all the shooting's stopped?"

Todd Harlon looked at Will as though he were mad. "Why, of course! It's the only time it's safe."

"Well, you'd best disperse this crowd while I get this young man up to the doctor's," Will ordered as he helped Bill Hardy to his feet. Somehow, he didn't think a man like Todd Harlon would know what to do in a situation like this, and he was right.

Up in Doc Miles's operating room, they lay a still conscious Bill Hardy down on the table that had recently been occupied by Jake, who was no longer in need of operating on. The undertaker would be his next stop, as would the body of Kyle Garret.

"Say, I'm mighty grateful for you coming along when you did, Bill," the lawman said, calling the young man by his first name. "But how'd you get here so soon? I thought I left you in a passel of dust back there with the horses?"

Hardy tried to smile as the doctor probed for the bullet just below his shoulder. "I come across a couple of boys who was looking for some stray calves. Told 'em I'd give 'em a dollar if they could bring that string of horses into Curious. Had to explain to 'em that the corpses wasn't nothing more than a handful of dead meat and wouldn't give 'em any lip. They should be here directly."

Will smiled at the lad, who seemed close to unconsciousness now, likely from loss of blood.

"What's the matter, Marshal? I do something wrong?"

"Not hardly, son. Why, you done and said all the right things out there."

"Then what you smiling at?"

"Just remembering what a young gambler said to me a day or two back."

"Oh?"

"Yeah. You're a real piece of work, Bill Hardy. A real piece of work."

And that was when Bill Hardy passed out.

CHAPTER

★ 26 ★

There are some days a body will get up and know, just know, that something important will happen that day before the sun sets. It was one of those days for Joshua Holly. The idea that he would be involved in something that could very well change the course of many a life in Twin Rifles had been stuck in the back of his mind ever since he'd gotten out of bed today. But for the life of him, he couldn't figure out what it was.

"Well, good morning, stranger," Sarah Ann said with a smile as he entered the Porter Cafe to take his breakfast. Normally he spent his time eating with Will Carston at the Ferris House, but this morning he had decided to try the Porter Cafe. Run by Big John Porter, the Porter Cafe was about the only true restaurant the town of Twin Rifles had. And it served food just as tasty as that served in the Ferris House. Of course, the thing about eating in either one of these establishments was that you had a good-looking woman to wait on you and serve your food. And Sarah Ann—Big John's daughter and the wife of Wash Carston, one of Will's boys—and Margaret and Rachel Ferris, why, they had to be the best looking women in town, don't you know?

"I thought you took most of your meals with Papa Will over at Margaret's establishment," Sarah Ann said as she pulled out her order pad and positioned her pencil. With blue eyes and truly blond hair, Joshua had always thought she was a real looker and couldn't blame young Wash Carston at all for marrying her a while back.

"Now that's the truth, Miss Sarah Ann," Joshua replied, tossing his hat on the empty seat next to him. "But something tells me that Regret feller over to Miss Margaret's is got hisself something up his sleeve besides his arm and shirt, if you know what I mean. And that sun coming up this morning, why, it was so beauteous coming up like it was . . . well, I just figured I'd start my day off visiting one of the best looking young ladies in this here town instead of some plug ugly like that Regret feller." Joshua gave her a wink and a smile upon finishing speaking.

Sarah Ann blushed as she said, "Why, Joshua, I do believe you're trying to flatter me just for an extra plate of food."

"Now ain't that the dangedest thing," Joshua said in mock anger. "Why, ever time I pay a woman a compliment they figures I'm a-trying to wheedle some extry food outta 'em."

Sarah Ann cocked a playful eye at the deputy. "Well, aren't you?"

It wasn't that Joshua was a beggar or anything so much as the fact that he never could shy away from the truth that well. "Now that you mention it, ma'am, a taste of your fine gravy over the taters and mebbe an extry biscuit and egg and piece of meat wouldn't harm me none. Keep away the hungers for the morning, don't you know?"

"You're incorrigible, Joshua," Sarah Ann laughed.

For the moment the deputy looked puzzled. "I ain't never heard that word afore, ma'am," he said. "Is that some high falooting cuss word you heard your daddy use, or what?"

"In your case, it's a compliment, Joshua," she said. "Besides, you know good and well I'd never cuss a man like you."

"Hmm." Joshua rubbing his jaw in thought, still a bit confused at the new word he'd heard this young lady use on him. "I'm gonna have to ask Will about that."

Joshua's eating habits showed no real preference for food. Both Sarah Ann and the Ferris women had discovered that if you put it on a plate and called it food, the Deputy Marshal would eat it, no matter how it tasted. So Sarah Ann took Joshua's order, which she knew by heart, and turned it over to Big John for preparation. A "mess of eggs and taters, a heap of biscuits and a thick slab of whatever meat you're fixing for the day," was how the deputy had once described what he might want for a breakfast meal. And, like the eating habits of the Carston men, Sarah Ann had definitely remembered this one too.

Joshua was joined halfway through his meal by Emmett, who had come to town early to check on whether Will Carston had gotten back with his horses yet. He placed an order for only coffee with Sarah

Ann, having already eaten an early breakfast at his small ranch.

"Don't you worry none 'bout Will, Mr. Emmett," Joshua said in his more reassuring manner. "He'll be back soon. Why, I can near feel it in my bones, don't you know? And he'll have your horses too. Ever lickety split one of 'em. Why, I'd guarantee it, that's how sure I am of it!"

"I don't know, Joshua, it just seems like an awful long—"

"Now, that goes to show how much you know 'bout the law, Emmett," the deputy said pointing a fork at the man as though he were taking aim to stab him with it. "Why, they's no telling how far Will's had to chase them horse thieves. Coulder gone up to the Nations, or all the way down to Mexico City, or mebbe even out west to them Staked Plains. Good Lord, I still hear old Chance ragging on 'bout that cattle drive he and Wash was on—"

"Yeah, I know," Emmett said, having been on the drive with Chance, although Joshua was sure that underneath it all the man seemed downright worried about the situation. "It's just that the whole thing is getting me itchy. I need something to do. Hell, I can't do a helluva lot out on the ranch without them horses."

Joshua smiled as he rose from the table, fumbled inside a pocket and pulled out a coin which he deposited on the table in payment for the meal. "And you ain't a-gonna do nothing afoot ary they's a horse about, right?"

"Damn right!" Emmett said with what Joshua was sure could only be false bravado.

Both men headed for the door now. "Don't you go a-worrying 'bout nothing a-tall, Emmett. Why, ever'thing's gonner be jest fine, I tell you," Joshua was saying as they left the Porter Cafe.

It was when they had stepped out onto the boardwalk that they stopped dead in their tracks, both of them. For there before them, in the middle of the street, was Ransome Regret. Facing Joshua and Emmett, a man would have to be blind not to notice that Regret was carrying a six-gun in his waistband and from the scowl on his face he looked like he was ready to use it. Carny and Wilson Hadley stood one on each side of him. They too were armed.

"Well now, lookee here, will you," Joshua said mildly. "You some kind of committee of three or are you jest standing there a-blocking traffic?"

"It's about time you were taught a lesson, Deputy," Regret snarled.

"Well, I hope you didn't bring these two knotheads along as your assistants," Joshua said, nodding to each of the Hadley brothers.

"And what's wrong with that?"

"Why, fiddle, ever'body knows they ain't got the brains God give a jackass, and that's putting it on the complimentary side!" Joshua said, flaying one hand off to the side for emphasis.

"You watch your mouth, Joshua, 'cause you're in big trouble," Carny said, acting as mean as he could muster, which wasn't hard for a Hadley at all.

"Don't tell me, let me guess," the deputy said, taking a step off the boardwalk and toward Regret. Emmett moved right along with him, as though he were the man's shadow. "Regret here's gonna get you two to do his fighting for him, is that it?"

"Boots 'n' saddles, boys!" Emmett said in a yell loud enough to wake the entire town. With a good deal of joy, he added, "I do believe I've found the scratch for my itch!"

"Do you know what this lopsided, two faced jackass has been doing in this town!" Joshua all but yelled at Carny.

"Just like I told you, Hadley, he's been harassing me!" Regret said in a voice that was none too convincing.

"Harass, my ass!" Joshua said, now filled with rage. He moved as he spoke and by the time he'd gotten his three words out he had taken two more big strides and swung on Ransome Regret, knocking him flat on his back with a big roundhouse right. "Now that's harassment!" he concluded with a nod and placed his hands on his hips as though he were a disgruntled parent expressing concern over a loudmouthed child's behavior.

The Hadley's were now giving one another cautious glances, not at all sure they had come to the right party.

"What's all the fuss about?" a sleepy eyed Dallas Bodeen said, making his way to the center of the street, pulling first one suspender then the other up over a shoulder. "Man can't even get any sleep around here."

"I was about to tell 'em what this Regret feller here's been doing to Miss Margaret, how he's tormenting her and all," the deputy said.

"Miss Margaret?" Carny asked, now thoroughly puzzled. Glaring down at Regret, who was sitting there rubbing his jaw, he said, "You didn't say nothing about that, did you?"

"Son?" Dallas said and Carny turned back toward him.

"Yeah?"

Dallas spit a gob of tobacco juice in Carny's eye, causing the older Hadley to bring his hands up to his face. In that one swift instant, Dallas took a step in toward Carny and lifted his six-gun from its holster.

"What did you do that for!" Carny asked, now angry himself as he wiped the spit off his face.

"It's too goddamn early to fight, so maybe I'll just shoot you instead," Dallas growled impatiently. "Unless, of course, you want to keep that trap of yours shut until you leave town."

At the same time Dallas made his move, Emmett decided to scratch his itch. He stepped into Wilson Hadley and hit him a hard right, knocking him back a step or two. It was followed with a left jab and another right that put Wilson on his back. When he started to try and get to his feet, he stopped real quick, noticing Emmett's foot square on his elsewheres.

"I wouldn't do that less'n you want to talk like some of the girls in this community when you get back on your feet," Emmett said with a sly grin. Wilson knew the big ex-cavalryman was just waiting for him to make such a foolish move.

"Now, you boys jest take my advice and head on back to your shack," Joshua continued, as though nothing had happened to stop the speech he was giving the Hadley Brothers. "Why, Miss Margaret finds out you been a-helping this fool, Regret, I'll guarantee you she won't feed you for a year. Or more!"

"The damn fools won't get nothing outta my cafe either," Big John Porter said in an emphatic manner, now standing at the entrance to his cafe, the ever present cleaver in his hand.

Joshua had turned to look over his shoulder at the

sight of Big John, momentarily forgetting the man sitting upright on the ground before him. Which was when Ransome Regret took the chance he had been waiting for.

He drew his six-gun, pulling it from his waistband, cocked it and took aim at Joshua's side. But the hammer only let out a loud click when he pulled the trigger. At first he had a sense of awe about him when he gazed bewildered at the malfunctioning weapon.

"Gotcha!" Joshua said, a confident grin on his face as he looked down at Regret, who was now aiming a second time at him. The tinhorn went through the motions a second time, the results also ending in a loud click.

"What the hell!" Regret said as he cocked the weapon a third time. Although he wanted to shoot the deputy in the worst way, he by now felt foolish. Perhaps this was why he only held the pistol in a half-hearted manner when he tried to shoot it the third time.

The gun bucked in explosion, rearing back in Regret's hand, its bullet sending Joshua's hat flying off into space. The stunned deputy did what he would have done the first time with any man holding a gun in Regret's position. He kicked it out of Regret's hand, the gun flying up and over into a nearby water trough, landing with a splash.

"You sorry ass cur," Joshua growled, truly mad now as he bent down with one hand and hauled Regret to his feet. On his feet, Regret was nothing more than a rag doll, Joshua slapping him around as hard as he could, so hard in fact that the man was near unconscious by the time Emmett placed a hand on the deputy's shoulder to stop him.

"Easy now, Joshua," Emmett said, trying to sound

soothing and knowing he was doing a damn poor job of it. "You kill him now, why, it'll take all the fun outta it. And you don't want to go to jail for that, do you?"

"I reckon we'd better be getting back home, folks," Carny Hadley said, embarrassed as could be. "Come on, Wilson, these good folks don't need us around here."

"And amen to that," Dallas said, slowly placing Carny's six-gun back in his holster. To Porter, he asked, "Ain't old Blacksnake Hank 'bout due to ride through for a stop, Big John?"

"That's a fact, Dallas," the big cafe owner said once he'd consulted his pocket watch. "Half an hour by my timepiece."

"Now, I know old Hank is partial to having riffraff on his stagecoach, but maybe ary you said a few words to him about Mr. Regret here—"

It only took Big John two long strides to reach Joshua, who was still holding Regret like some rag doll. Grabbing the half-conscious man from Joshua's grasp, he half-pushed, half-carried him over to the boardwalk and plunked him down in a chair.

With a huge grin, he looked down at the stunned Ransome Regret. "Don't worry, Dallas, he'll listen to me," Big John said. "Everybody listens to me." It wasn't that the big man was arrogant, he was simply stating a known fact. To Regret he said in a loud voice, "Move from that chair and I'll make son-of-a-bitch stew out of you."

And that was that, as far as Ransome Regret was concerned.

Margaret Ferris appeared out of nowhere, having taken in all that had happened and by now filled with emotion. She approached the group of men, dabbing her eyes with the tip of her apron. She gently kissed Joshua on the cheek and the man almost fell over.

"Woman's crazed, I tell you," Dallas said, just as befuddled as the deputy. "Done the very same thing to me, a day or so back."

"You've all done so much I don't now where to begin, or how to repay you," a tearful Margaret said.

"Now you know better than that, ma'am," Emmett said, his hat off in the woman's presence. "If we don't help one another in this land, why, we wouldn't be able to depend on no one."

"Thank you, Mr. Emmett," Margaret said in a soft tone. "I'll be forever grateful to you for ridding my life of Ransome Regret." She paused for a moment, as though to gather her thoughts. "But there is one other thing I have to ask you, one other favor. And I'm afraid it's a big one."

"Why shoot, ma'am, don't jest stand there," Joshua said insistently. "Spit it out, git it off'n your chest." Turning suddenly red in the face, he added in a sheepish manner, "Begging your pardon, ma'am."

So Margaret Ferris spoke and they heard her out.

And she got her wish.

CHAPTER

★ 27 ★

It took a couple of days for young Bill Hardy to feel like he was well enough to get up and move about while his wound healed. And it was during that time that Will Carston made sure Todd Harlon made positive identifications of Kyle Garret and his henchmen. Once this was taken care of, Will made sure the City Marshal of Curious wired the proper authorities for the reward money on those members of the outlaw gang who had prices over their heads, and there were several of them who did.

As for his own flesh wound, Doc Miles said it turned out to be only lightly infected and treated and wrapped it before telling the lawman he was free to go as long as he didn't do much in the way of strenuous movement with his left arm.

After his fourth day of recuperation, Will asked Hardy if he had any plans to return to Twin Rifles for a visit.

"No, I think I'll stick around here for a while, Marshal," was the young gambler's reply. "Besides, I've got to get that other horse of the farmer's and take it back out to him once I feel a mite better."

"Well, I'll be leaving tomorrow then," Will said in a matter-of-fact manner. "Be taking Emmett's horses back to him now that I've got 'em." He then went on to explain how he had convinced Todd Harlon to do the proper thing in clearing the way for his reward money. "Oughtta be here by the time the week is out, by my line of thought," Will added. "A thousand dollars or more, I'm figuring. That's quite a claim to stake."

"You take care of yourself, Bill," the lawman said the next morning after the two had eaten a big breakfast together in a local eatery. "You come in right handy in a tight spot toward the end there."

Hardy nodded with a slight smile, saying, "A man could really learn a lot just being around you, Marshal. You're a real knowledgeable man. I know I learned a lot."

Will thanked him for the compliment, mounted his horse and led Emmett's horses on the trail back to Twin Rifles and the Emmett ranch house.

Will took his time getting back to where he'd come from, taking a good three days of peaceful riding to get to Emmett's ranch house, where he turned the horses over to the ex-cavalryman. Then, riding an easy lope, he rode into Twin Rifles, where he arrived late one afternoon.

"Well, golly be, would you lookee here," Joshua said as he pulled up in front of his office and jail.

"Why, you made it back after all, Will. You know, you sure had old Emmett worried some a few days back. Why, he wasn't shore you hadn't took his breed and headed for the Canadian border, to hear him talk."

"So I heard," Will said and explained that he had just come from the Emmett spread and the delivery of Emmett's horses.

"But where's them horse thieves, Will? Don't you usually bring back a whole string of 'em draped across they saddles?"

"Buried 'em before coming home this time, old hoss," Will said, only half in jest. Joshua wouldn't find out until later that the bodies of Kyle Garret and his gang were being laid to rest in the boot hill graveyard in the small town of Curious, where the people weren't really interested at all in the goings-on of their town.

Dallas Bodeen made his way down the street about then, having seen Will enter town and pull up in front of the jail. He had a big grin on his face as he shook the marshal's hand and welcomed him home.

"Well, what's been going on since I was gone?" Will finally asked, as both men knew he would.

"Why, absolutely nothing, Will. Absolutely nothing," Joshua said. "It's been quiet as could be, it has."

Dallas snorted, adding, "Quiet ain't the word for it, Will. Why, it's been deader'n an undertaker's showroom. Believe me, you didn't miss a thing." He gave Will a slap on the back and said, "Come on, I'll buy you a beer over to Ernie Johnson's. Then we can have supper over at the Ferris House. You just know Miss Margaret is a-gonna want to see you again."

On the way over to Ernie Johnson's Saloon, Will felt a certain amount of reassurance in knowing that he could leave the town of Twin Rifles and not have to worry about anything significant taking place. It was a comforting feeling and he liked it.

Once he'd walked through the front door of the Ferris House for supper and Margaret Ferris noticed him, she dragged him over to the living room area where no one was located at the moment, and gave him a big kiss. Will responded in kind, telling her he had missed her terribly.

After supper Will and Margaret had taken seats out on the veranda and talked until the sun set. It was when Will began yawning that she led him to his room upstairs. There was only a little light from the hallway that shone in the room once Will was in it, but it was all they needed.

They kissed silently in the dark then, small but meaningful kisses at first, gradually longer and more passionate as they held one another. When Margaret finally left his embrace, she closed and locked the door to his room.

"You know, Will, I'll bet its been some time since you've seen a woman naked," she whispered to him as she began to unbutton his shirt.

At first Will didn't know what to do, but then he said, "Do you mean naked, or nekkid?"

"What's the difference?" Margaret asked inquisitively.

"Well, a person who is naked is just that, they got no clothes on."

"And nekkid?"

Will smiled in the dark. "That means you ain't got no clothes on but you're having fun at it," he chuckled.

Then they kissed again with all the warmth and

passion of two people who genuinely do love one another.

And if you asked Will Carston what happened next, he would likely give you an answer that could come from only Will Carston:

"NONE OF YOUR GODDAMN BUSINESS!"

Printed in the United States
By Bookmasters